A Subtle Dragon

A SUBTLE DRAGON

Dragons of Mayfair Book 3

E.B. WHEELER

Rowan Ridge
Press

Print ISBN: 978-173604-1-154

First printing: April 2022

Published by Rowan Ridge Press, Utah

Cover and interior design © Rowan Ridge Press

Front cover image by Onesketchman based on "Mrs. Robert Dickey (Anne Brown)" by John Wesley Jarvis.

Back cover image "The Burning of the Houses of Lords and Commons" by J.M.W. Turner.

❀ Created with Vellum

For everyone who lifts up a light in dark times and dark places

Chapter One

It was a Tuesday the first time someone tried to kill Lady Amelia Chase.

She was walking in Hyde Park with Lady Phoebe Westing after a shopping excursion to order new gowns for Phoebe's Interesting Condition. Phoebe had sent her footman home with an armful of fabrics for the nursery, so only Brainy Jamie, the faithful street urchin Phoebe had taken in, was left to escort the two ladies.

The lad strolled in front of them, his chest puffed with importance as they circled the Park in a slow parade with the rest of the *haut ton*. Amelia smiled at the way Jamie scrutinized the passing Corinthians with their champagne-polished Hessian boots and the ladies whose bonnets bore enough flowers to supply an army of florists.

"A light-fingered lad could pick plenty 'o blunt amongst all these swells," Jamie announced to the ladies.

"Jamie!" Phoebe exclaimed. "I hope that doesn't mean what I think it does."

Jamie turned on his most innocent smile. "Don't fret, m'lady. I'm on the straight 'n narrow now, thanks to you."

Amelia snickered. Phoebe shook her head and turned her attention back to Amelia.

"I finished Miss Charity's latest book," Phoebe said, stroking the green dragon perched on her shoulder. A few flashes of light blinked above Phoebe, her magic slipping through in her excitement. "It's her best yet. Very thrilling, with lovers' trysts and traitors in the court. Have you read it?"

"I have." Amelia dodged the leavings of a horse, careful to keep her skirts clear of the mess. Her father wouldn't give her an allowance for new gowns. After all, this was her third Season, and it seemed clear that she wasn't going to take. An old family name was not much of an enticement anymore without old money to go with it, and Amelia wasn't even dragon-linked. Men looked over her fiery red hair and wry expression and then quickly looked elsewhere.

So, she would enjoy the variety of London one last time, then be banished to keep some old maiden aunt company in the country, sequestered away with the antique furniture that was too ugly to use but too traditional to be rid of. But it might not be such a disaster. Perhaps the aunt would like to gossip and play cards.

"I often suspect you are not a favorite of hers, either," Phoebe said.

Amelia shook her head. "I beg your pardon. I think I missed the context." She knew her friend wasn't talking about the hypothetical aunt, but it was hard to keep up with conversation over the clatter of hooves and babble of overly-cheery voices calling friends.

"Miss Charity," Phoebe said apologetically. "In her latest book, I thought your character seemed a bit... dull?" She quickly added, "I don't think she's well-acquainted with you, though, because I know you to have a keen wit."

What dreadful words, so loaded with expectation, especially when all Amelia could think to say was, "Oh, I'm glad you find it so. Much of London does not appreciate it, I'm afraid."

Was her character in Miss Charity's books dull? She hadn't thought much about it. The books were a parody of King Arthur's court, but it was not hard to spot the resemblances of the fictional characters to members of London's *haut ton*. Therein lay the secret to their popularity; the stories were rather silly and melodramatic, but who could resist a good gossip?

"Who do you suppose she is?" Phoebe asked, her gaze darting

around the park as if she suspected to spot the mysterious authoress lurking behind one of the trees, taking notes on them.

The scarlet coat of a letter carrier caught Amelia's attention. His ringing bell blended with the jangle of harnesses and chirping of birds in the Park. Amelia felt for the pocket under her skirts, and the paper hidden there crinkled. She'd been searching for an opportunity to be rid of the letter without Phoebe or anyone else noticing. If its contents were known, it would be her social ruin.

"Watch out!" Brainy Jamie shouted.

A chestnut mare bolted toward them over the green, defying the orderly parade of the Park. Amelia's first thought was that some foolish lad had let his horse get out of control, but, no, he drove his horse directly at her and Phoebe, as dandies swooned and ladies in delicate muslin gowns leapt out of the way.

Amelia grabbed Phoebe's arms and swung her out of the rider's path.

A sharp sting radiated from the side of Amelia's head, and her ear rung. She spun to find herself facing the rider, his whip raised.

Phoebe cradled her belly, her face pale but defiant, while her dragon hissed and flared his wings.

Was this another attack by the anti-magic Luddites against the dragon-linked?

Amelia kept herself between Phoebe and the rider. A white bauta mask covered his face, dark eye holes staring out from the smooth, featureless angles of the disguise. Amelia stared at the eerie, unknowable face and wondered if this was Shaw himself, the ruthless leader of the Luddites.

But the rider ignored Phoebe and her dragon, dropping his whip and raising a pistol to aim at Amelia's chest. Everything slowed to a standstill. Her breath came fast and shallow, and her quickening heartbeat thrummed in her ears. She saw nothing but the gaping black end of the weapon. She couldn't move, just waited for the blast that would kill her. She thought abstractly that her mother would be furious with her dying in such an unladylike manner. And they would find the letter on her body. How awkward.

A blinding flash of light from behind Amelia struck the rider full in the face. Phoebe's magic. The horse shrieked and reared. Amelia scrambled aside, rubbing at the spots swimming over her eyes and willing her sight to return.

The rider swore. The pistol fired, and Amelia winced at the shattering boom, but nothing struck her.

A prickling sensation crawled over her skin, and the sudden scent of storm clouds rolled over her. She blinked hard and made out the figure of the young woman striding down the path, arms outstretched like some ancient goddess of storm and sky. A pale-yellow dragon with undertones of silver rode on her shoulder. It was Deborah Shaw, the niece of the Luddite leader, who had recently come out of hiding to take a stand against her uncle's co-conspirators.

"Deborah!" Phoebe called. "Not in the Park. All these people!"

Deborah pointed at the rider. "Begone, foul wretch!" Her hair rose from its curls, giving her a golden halo. Her dragon flapped its wings to glide above her. And though the day had been clear before, thunder rumbled in the distance. "Tell my uncle the Luddites are not welcome in London."

Whether the rider was one of Shaw's Luddites or not, he had no stomach for facing an over-dramatic young woman attuned to lightning. He wheeled his mount and charged back out of the Park.

"I say, that was impressive." Max Hart, Phoebe's brother, ran up to put an arm around Deborah's shoulders. Amelia's vision had cleared enough to catch the treacle-sweet, lovesick look the two exchanged. She rolled her eyes.

Max turned his attention to his sister. "Phoebs! Did that villain harm you?"

Phoebe shook her head. "Lady Amelia saved me. Oh, dear, your ear is bleeding!"

Amelia reached up to her throbbing ear, and her fingers came away sticky.

"Here, now," purred a deep male voice behind Amelia. "Someone get her a handkerchief before the blood ruins her dress as well."

Phoebe scrambled in her chatelaine for a handkerchief, but as Amelia turned an exasperated look on the Earl of Blackerby, she found that he already held one out for her. The shadows that followed in his wake, weak now under the bright springtime sun, pooled around his feet like an over-sized cloak. His dark gray dragon perched on his shoulder, watching Amelia with hard, black eyes.

"Thank you, my lord," she said, taking the handkerchief warily.

Lord Blackerby, Secretary of the Home Office, attuned to darkness, never did anything for just one reason. He also had a knack for appearing when there was trouble. Whether that was due to his magic or something else, Amelia didn't know.

"Phoebe!" Lord Westing cut through the crowd, which was happy to part for the angry lord with the white-blond hair and the ice dragon. He embraced his wife. "I heard there was an accident?"

"I don't think it was," Phoebe said. "Lady Amelia put herself between myself and the man, and he attacked her."

Murmurs of shock rippled through the onlookers.

"And you were injured?" Lord Westing looked at Amelia with concern, though of course not with the fervor that he showed to his wife.

Amelia doubted anyone would ever look at her the way Lord Westing looked at his lady.

"And the villain ruined her bonnet!" Deborah added.

Several ladies in the crowd gasped.

Blackerby stepped forward. "The question remains, Lady Amelia: who would wish to harm such a charming lady as yourself?"

"I believe it is your business to discover that, my lord."

He bowed with a sardonic grin. "And so, I have the privilege of questioning the lovely witnesses. Do you have any idea who it was?"

"He wore a bauta mask, so I couldn't see much of him. His horse was a chestnut."

"Yes," Blackerby said with a dismissive wave. "He abandoned it just outside the Park. My Runners are tracking down its owner, but I believe it to be a hired hack. Anything else?"

Amelia shook her head, bouncing some of her coppery curls loose. "I thought at first it might be a Luddite or...or even Shaw," she added in a low voice. "But he was at least as intent on attacking me as Lady Westing. Though, we did go to Mrs. Reynolds' shop earlier."

"Ah," Blackerby said.

Mrs. Reynolds was one of the few dragon-linked who chose not to join Society, making gowns for its ladies instead. But she was attuned to fire, and when Luddites attacked her shop the previous Season, she had unleashed fire in the streets. It had not helped the undercurrent of anti-magic sentiment.

"What do you make of it, then?" Westing snapped at Blackerby.

"My dear Lord Westing, I have no idea. Yet. Except that we must do what we can to make the streets safe again. These Luddites have become far too troublesome."

"Indeed," Westing agreed. "I will see the ladies home."

"In fact, I would like the privilege of escorting Lady Amelia," Blackerby said. "The miscreant who attacked her is still at large, and she may draw him out again."

Westing gave Blackerby an exasperated look, then had the courtesy to turn to Amelia for her opinion.

"I have no desire to be bait in your trap, my lord," she said to Blackerby. "And I had other errands I wished to complete today."

"Oh, excellent. I'll escort you, then. The more you wander about, the more chance there is that that deranged fellow will return, and I do so wish to meet him."

That would not do at all. Everyone was already staring at them, and Blackerby and his pet shadows would only make that worse. She would have no chance to be rid of the letter, which now felt even more pressing. Blackerby ferreted out secrets like a bloodhound. Furthermore, her father, the Marquess of Hayes, did not like their family to draw attention. It was vulgar. He did not like the Earl of Blackerby, either—also vulgar, at least by her father's standards. So, whatever she did, she was going to incur her father's wrath.

Amelia glowered at Blackerby. "If I must have your company, then home it is."

He grinned. "I'm so glad you're reasonable."

Blackerby didn't offer her a ride in his carriage, instead walking her the short distance to Grosvenor Square. She kept up a quick, annoyed gait, but Blackerby's long stride allowed him to match pace with her. The ever-present shadows swirled behind him, and his dragon sailed above, its long neck turning to and fro as it surveyed the streets of

Mayfair. For Luddite dangers, Amelia hoped, though perhaps it was hunting out secrets for its master. Amelia did not know how close the link was between human and animal. One of the things she missed out on by not being dragon-linked. Of course, until this very day, she'd never been troubled by miscreants either.

It didn't take long to reach her family's house in Grosvenor Square. Iron railings warded off intruders. The stairs took them to the front door, passing the sunken windows of the servants' area below like drawbridge over a moat. The nobility had brought their castles with them when they moved to London's fashionable streets and squares, tradition etched into every stone. Amelia felt a moment of dread at the thought being locked inside, despite the safety. That was the problem with moats and drawbridges: they didn't just keep people out, they also kept them in.

When they reached the door, Amelia turned to Blackerby. "Thank you for seeing to my safety. You may go."

His eyes twinkled with amusement. "Oh, no, I should see you inside."

"You know perfectly well—"

But her father's butler, Moore, was too prompt. He opened the door and announced, "The Earl of Blackerby and Lady Amelia, ma'am."

Lady Hayes stood in the foyer, arranging flowers in a vase.

"Amelia! Was that you making that noise outside the door?" Lady Hayes' hand fluttered to her chest. "My goodness, what happened to you?"

"A horseman nearly ran me down in the Park." Amelia wanted to downplay the incident, but she couldn't disguise the fact that her ear was bleeding. "His whip hit me."

Lady Hayes wrinkled her nose and stepped back, putting some distance between herself and her daughter. "What an ordeal! Your father will be upset to hear it."

"No doubt," Amelia said.

"You should know it well. It was very plebeian of you to be mixed up in that sort of adventure. And in Hyde Park, where everyone might see! Not at all in keeping with our station."

"I shall try to recall my station next time someone threatens to run me down," Amelia said with a straight face.

Her mother studied her for a moment, obviously trying to decide if she was serious. "Well, it would be better not to be run down at all."

"Excellent advice, Lady Hayes," Lord Blackerby said. He bowed to Amelia. "I'm sure I shall see you again quite soon."

Amelia inclined her head coldly. She found Blackerby's—Promise? Threat?—almost as disconcerting as the attack in the Park, or her father's forthcoming diatribe on the subject. She sighed and patted the chatelaine pouch pinned to her waistband to be sure the incriminating letter was still safe. Then she went upstairs to change. A bit of blood had dropped onto the delicate, puffed shoulder of her gown after all.

Chapter Two

AMELIA HANDED her dress over to her maid, Jane, with apologies for the bloodstain. The girl looked delightedly shocked as she took the dress, no doubt excited for the interest the gossip would create for all the servants below stairs. Amelia silently wished them joy in the momentary relief from boredom.

With the maid gone, she turned her attention back to the letter she'd never had a chance to deliver. She sat at her writing table and tapped the edge of the letter on the worn wood. Perhaps she should arrange a visit to her cousin Mrs. Jonston in Fleet Street. Normally, her mother would allow her to hire a carriage and take a footman on such "charitable" visits, but Amelia had a feeling her mother would be more restrictive after the attack in Hyde Park. Not out of a particular concern for Amelia's safety. Her mother dwelt in a serene fantasy where the worst that ever happened to old families like theirs were substandard marriages and gambling debts. No, it was the interest—the scandal—that would make her mother hesitate. She wouldn't want common people on the street to gossip about a member of the Chase family.

Amelia glanced down at the square below and observed a little street sweep with his broom, entreating the passing ladies and gentlemen to employ his services. Occasionally, someone would toss him a coin, and he would run ahead of them to clear their path. Amelia had no romantic notions about his difficult life, but she did envy his freedom of movement.

Dinnertime allowed her at least to exit her bedchamber. She walked downstairs, composed to listen to her father's lecture on propriety with complacency. But she heard the sounds of unfamiliar male voices, and her heart fluttered in relief. Her father would never air family business in front of visitors. Must put on a good face for the world.

When she entered the dining room, she paused and squeezed her eyes shut. Her father's visitors were Lord Jasper and Lord Blackerby. Lord Jasper was an undersecretary for the Alien Office, overseeing dangerous foreigners. Put him together with Blackerby from the Home Office, and this was not a casual visit. Amelia began to think she would prefer her father's lecture.

Blackerby nodded when he caught her gaze, his lip curled in that smirk of his. His dragon strode over and sniffed the hem of her dress, then allowed her to scratch behind the small horns on his head. Blackerby followed.

"He doesn't take to many people," Blackerby said to her in a low voice.

"I've always been fond of animals," Amelia said, far too aware that her father was watching her. Would he take exception to her daring to speak to Blackerby? Or would he decide to try to force a match between them? Either option was more trouble for her.

Blackerby smiled that too-knowing smile of his. "Shade likes people with secrets."

Amelia raised an eyebrow. "Then he must like everyone. Who doesn't have secrets?"

"Touché, Lady Amelia." Blackerby bowed to her, and his dragon hopped back onto his shoulder. But when Blackerby walked away, the dragon turned to watch her. It gave Amelia an uneasy feeling, like the dragon was gazing into her mind. Dragons couldn't do that, could they? Blackerby couldn't, she hoped.

During dinner, the visitors revealed their motivations for visiting. They discussed the rising Luddite threats—attacks in the north, rumors of conspiracies in London. Thankfully, they did not mention the attack in Hyde Park, as that would have brought Amelia into the midst of it. She was back on the outside, as she had been the last time Shaw had been in London. Or with the incident of the water dragon in Lyme Regis. Or, truthfully, nearly anywhere she went. Just watching from the edges.

"Even Prinny is concerned about the Luddites," Blackerby said.

Amelia winced a little, and her father sniffed disdainfully.

"I find it disrespectful to call the Prince Regent 'Prinny,'" he said.

"I don't," Blackerby replied.

"You are an earl," Hayes said, "But that does not mean you are above reproach. I am a marquess, remember. I have royal ancestors, and my family predates yours by a century."

"Oh, at least," Blackerby said, not trying to repress his smile. "You are an antiquity."

Lord Hayes' eyes narrowed. "You should not disdain to take advice from those with more experience."

"I take whatever advice suits me, my lord."

Her father's face turned red with fury. Amelia ducked her head and stirred the wine sauce around her plate with a piece of duck. This was going to be an unpleasant night.

"To the point," Lord Jasper said quickly, "we fear there may be members of Society who have joined the Luddite cause."

"Poppycock!" Lord Hayes exclaimed. "No one of breeding would ever do such a foolish thing. It's only a Luddite rumor to sow dissension in the ranks."

Amelia rubbed her eyes so she wouldn't roll them. It was a sore spot with her father that no one in the family had been dragon-linked for generations, and that "unknowns" were popping up with dragons. Yet he would never dream of turning on dragons, since they had been a sign of power and divine favor for generations. He would also never be able to imagine anyone thinking differently than he did, except the incomprehensible "riffraff."

Lord Blackerby looked about to say something snide, but Lord Jasper rushed to cut him off. "That may be the case, but we want to keep our allies in Parliament informed of the situation."

"Ah," Lord Hayes said. "Of course. We should come down harder on these rabble rousers. Transportation is the answer! Send them to America."

Lord Jasper cleared his throat, and Blackerby jumped in with a wicked grin. "The Americans might object—they're not our colony anymore."

"Even if we sent them to *Australia*," Lord Jasper jumped in, "it wouldn't discourage people from being Luddites."

Lady Hayes set her napkin aside with a stiff smile. "We ladies should leave and allow the men their political discussion. This doesn't concern us, Amelia."

Amelia found, in fact, that it concerned her very much, but she would not make a scene, so she rose from the table with her mother. The men stood as they left the room, then resumed their discussion, trying to solve ticklish problems like how to keep people from killing one another.

As Amelia picked up some needlework beside her mother in the red drawing room, she couldn't help thinking about possible solutions. Anything diplomatic, however, was out of the question as long as Shaw was at large. The Luddites might be happy with more protections for workers—reassurances that magic would not replace their employment—or more say in the government whether or not they had dragons. But that wasn't enough for Shaw. He thought dragons and magic were abominations and wanted them eliminated. There was no negotiating with madness or fanaticism.

It was some time before the men finally joined them. Judging by Blackerby's smirk, Jasper's frown, and her father's immediate call for more wine—but not the good wine he saved for favored guests—Amelia guessed the discussion had not gone well. Her mother's attempts to draw the men into a game of cards fell flat.

"Amelia!" her father barked. "Play something for our guests."

Amelia obeyed, making her way to the harp in the corner and beginning the tedious process of tuning the strings.

"Not that racket," her father said. "Play a song."

Amelia repressed a deep sigh. It really would be a racket if she didn't tune the strings. Instead of trying to get a melody out of the half-tuned instrument, she played a series of arpeggios and glissandos, not as jarring if the notes were off. The music served its purpose: their guests could pretend to listen and save themselves the trouble of making awkward conversation. Blackerby, though, watched her with a glint of amusement in his eye. Just to punish him for paying attention, she purposely played some of the chords wrong. No one else noticed, but his eyes danced with suppressed laughter.

Amelia came to the end of a set of scales and rested her out-of-practice fingertips for a moment.

Lord Jasper, who had been staring out the window, said, "There is the littlest sweep I have ever seen out there. He's a sad figure."

Lord Hayes' lip curled up. "We should have him run off."

"That would be a shame," Amelia said without thinking. "He is excellent at his job, and no doubt his family needs the income."

"He is beneath your notice," her father reprimanded. "One sweep is the same as another."

Amelia wanted to argue, but then her father would just bluster at her all night, and it wouldn't accomplish anything, except perhaps to make him more determined to harass the boy.

Their guests departed not long after. Amelia used the confusion of their departure to head upstairs without dealing with her father. She glanced out her window at the square and was surprised to see Lord Blackerby strolling through the green space. It should not have surprised her; he lived close, if she recalled correctly. But he stopped the little sweep, spoke to him for a moment, and handed him a coin. Of course, the arrogant man wouldn't risk dirtying his boots. But she was a little pleased that he had chosen her little sweep for the job. Sometimes, Blackerby wasn't entirely obnoxious.

Blackerby tossed a shilling to David, the street sweep he had hired to watch the Chase house, and mentally thanked Phoebe Westing for giving him the idea when she took in Brainy Jamie. The city's urchins were a veritable army of spies, and it helped to have at least some of them in his employ.

Shade perched on his shoulder, and the shadows drawn to his attunement followed him. They always wanted to whisper their secrets. He had learned that listening could quickly drive a fellow mad.

He arrived home and handed off his coat and hat to his valet Crankshaw, then shut the study door on the man. Luckily, Crankshaw was used to Blackerby's moods. The ability to boast of being employed by the mysterious and mercurial—and always impeccable—Earl of Blackerby was apparently enough to offset the fact that being mysterious and mercurial also made one difficult to work for. Blackerby paid him well, too. It wouldn't do to have Crankshaw go elsewhere and spread any secrets.

That was Blackerby's job.

He hadn't gotten much from Lord Hayes. Not that he'd expected to. Hayes was one of the most disagreeable lords in Parliament, but he seemed very loyal, a worshiper of tradition—and dragons and their magic had belonged to aristocrats long before any of the "new blood" had begun to show up with their own dragons. The shadows in Hayes' house quavered with knowledge of his unkindness to everyone in his circle, as if even the darkness disliked him, but Blackerby sensed nothing treasonous. Shade had ignored the lord and lady as he did with those who were not harboring significant secrets.

Not Lady Amelia, though.

Blackerby sat at his desk and smiled to himself as he thought about how the red-headed lady's eyes flashed when he annoyed her. And she had secrets. He had almost made the mistake of forgetting that a lady could be a traitor as easily as a man. Unforgivable, at least in Blackerby's position. Lady Amelia had been at the party where the Luddites attacked last Season. She had also been on the coast where Shaw led his invasion. And she knew things. Blackerby recognized the look. A kindred spirit—unless, of course, she was working against their country instead of for it. It bore looking into. Blackerby didn't mind that part of his work. After all, he enjoyed parties, especially when there was someone interesting to talk to, or flirt with, or both.

Humming to himself, he sorted through his invitations, deciding which one he could expect to find the Lady Amelia attending. He lifted a card from Lady Greenley on behalf of her daughter, Lady Millicent Blanchfield. Perfect. For reasons unknown, Lady Amelia enjoyed the company of Lady Millicent. And rumors claimed that the less savory members of Society planned to attend the Greenley's party, no doubt drawn by the notorious bad habits of Lord Randolph Blanchfield. Perhaps even some rabble rousers. So, Blackerby would be attending—he examined the invitation more closely—

"Ah, that would explain it," he said with a chuckle. "What better place for secrets and conspiracies?"

Shade looked up at him with interest.

"Yes, my dear, we will be attending a costume ball."

Chapter Three

AMELIA WAS NOT FOND of attending balls. Her first Season, they had been exciting, but now, with her third Season under way, she was not often asked to dance, and she was not so generous-hearted that watching other people's merriment brought her much enjoyment. A costume ball, though: that had potential.

At any rate, it wasn't her choice. Her parents—and their views of what was proper—shaped the course of her life. It was only in small, secret rebellions that she could wrest away any control of her destiny.

Her family rarely interacted during the day, with her father always at his club and his mother finding things to do around the house that generally interfered with the servants' work. Only at the dinner table did they meet, and even then, it was sitting a distance from each other at the formal table. Amelia arrived just after her father and mother and took her place at the walnut table. The deep brown wood glowed in the candlelight, with any stains or scuffs buffed out so no one need know there had ever been an imperfection. Eventually, Amelia supposed, they would polish the table so thin that there would be nothing left of the wood, and the whole thing would collapse.

They ate the first course in silence, the only sound in the room the clinking of spoons against porcelain and the muffled steps of servants refilling glasses and clearing plates.

"The Greenleys are holding a costume ball," Lady Hayes said, her voice too loud in the quiet.

Lord Hayes grunted.

"I believe Amelia and I should attend. I shall be a shepherdess. Won't that be charming?"

Lord Hayes sniffed. "It sounds like a waste of money and effort, if you're thinking our daughter is more likely to catch a husband with her face covered. She still hasn't learned to be agreeable after two Seasons, and time is not improving her."

Amelia set her fork down, resisting the temptation to gouge a new mark into the table. She refused to look at either of her parents. She had heard variations of this argument too many times before. The words were scratched so deeply into her mind that she often heard them in her dreams.

"We cannot appear to think ourselves above Society by never going out," Lady Hayes said.

Lord Hayes wrinkled his nose. "If you must go then at least wear something fitting your station."

Lady Hayes frowned, then her face brightened again. "Oh, I shall dress as Marie Antoinette, as a memorial to the poor fallen queen."

Amelia thought that seemed in poor taste, but her father didn't object, so she had nothing to say that they would hear. Her mother would want to be seen. Amelia's costume, she decided, would be a better disguise. That, at least, would be amusing.

She would not be able to have a costume made, so she went through the old trunks where her mother had found a gown appropriate to the previous generation. Some of the colors were very bright. Amelia smiled at the idea that came to her and began sorting through the motley old clothes to create the perfect costume.

It took her several days to assemble her gown for the ball. She made certain her mother didn't know of her project until she descended the stairs when it was time to leave.

Lady Hayes gawked then leaned against the banister for support. "Oh, Amelia! What are you wearing?

Amelia twirled, letting her mother take in the full effect. She had taken apart a purple gown and a green one and sewn them back together, so her skirt was half one color and half the other. For the bodice, she had done the same but reversed the colors, with old-fashioned slits in the puffed sleeves showing the muslin she wore beneath. And with the extra fabric, she had patched together a jester's cap.

Her mother's forehead wrinkled behind the little domino mask that did not disguise her eyes. "A harlequin? I'm not sure your father would approve."

He would not. Amelia smiled. "But I don't have time to create something different. Think of this as an attempt to bring in the Venetian Carnival style. And at least I am not dressed as a milkmaid. Or as a man."

Her mother shuddered. "Very well. Let us be off. If I had not seen you come down the stairs, I would not know you for my daughter. Why, your hair is completely covered."

Amelia smiled to herself. That was the point. She tied the black domino mask over her eyes. This would be an enjoyable evening after all.

They took sedan chairs to the party, her father having disposed of his carriage for economy's sake, and her mother afraid to walk and spoil her gown.

The two men who lifted Amelia's chair were burly fellows. She felt a bit sorry for them, hauling ladies to parties all around Mayfair, but horses were so expensive to keep, as were grooms. Since her brother had married, their father had declared all of it unnecessary. He never went out, and the women could find their own way to parties.

A letter carrier walked past them, ringing his bell.

"Oh, stop, please!" Amelia called to the chairmen. "Please, let me out."

They did as she asked, and she scrambled out of the chair, fumbling in her pocket for the letter she had been anxious to be rid of. The letter carrier looked a bit taken back by Amelia's costume, but he accepted the letter.

She climbed back into the chair, and a warm feeling of relief settled over her as the chair lurched and set back into its bouncing, swaying rhythm. Amelia could have had her father frank the letter so the recipient didn't have to pay for the postage, but that would create a link to her family she could not afford. Especially with her costume, her anonymity was safe.

The chairmen deposited them in front of the Greenley's townhouse. The windows were lit with candles, and the sounds of merry voices drifted out to the street. Lady Hayes paid the chairmen, and Amelia followed her up the stairs.

To preserve the fun of the costumes, the guests were not announced. Lady Hayes, freed from the watchful eye of her husband, brightened up and found friends to talk with. Amelia quickly slipped away from her mother so she would not be identified. She toyed with her fan as she strolled the room. Her dress elicited many curious glances, some admiring, and she smiled. How novel it was to be seen but remain undetected.

There were Lord and Lady Westing dressed as… Amelia laughed to herself. Lord Westing was the Stone Knight and Phoebe the Lady of the Light from Miss Charity's books, complete with glowing magic orb. Some people pretended not to recognize themselves in the popular novels, but of course two such honest people would not shirk from their depictions. Their dragons perched on their shoulders, taking in the view of the room.

Lady Millicent was dressed as a peacock, obvious for her dragon—also wearing peacock feathers—as well as her thinly disguised face. She was flirting with someone. The French refugee Pierre Moreau. Amelia stepped closer, wondering if her friend would recognize her in her costume.

"An excellent idea, Lady Millicent, to hold a costume ball," Moreau said, his accent lending a musical cadence to his words. "It gives one the opportunity to wear something new." He held out his arms, displaying his blue coat dripping with lace in the old-fashioned style. "I am a musketeer, you see, ready to fight for love."

Millicent giggled. "Very charming."

"But not as charming as you, my lady."

"Ha!" Randolph Blanchfield interrupted his sister's flirtation. He wore only a domino mask—no costume—and his long neck meant he was one of the few men who could wear the high, starched collars in fashion without looking at least a little silly. "None of the Frenchmen I see in England are willing to fight for anything."

Moreau's eyes narrowed. "Give us something worth fighting for."

"Like love?" Randolph asked mockingly.

Millicent looked ready to defend Moreau, but her mother Lady Greenley drew her aside. Amelia was close enough to overhear her scolding.

"Really, Millicent, flirting with that Frenchman? You lower yourself. You must aim higher."

Amelia backed away, not wanting to hear more of the lecture.

It was easy enough for her to overhear all the latest *on-dits*. Eliza Prescott was married to her Captain Parry. Of course, Millicent wouldn't have invited Eliza to her party, but Amelia doubted Eliza cared, especially if she was newly married. Good for her. Not that there had been much doubt in the matter. Some people had the right cards dealt to them: beauty, fortune, a dragon. Amelia only had a courtesy title and connections to decaying gentility. Eliza Prescott was the future, and Amelia was the past.

Part of Amelia had been curious to hear what people had to say about her. But it seemed they said nothing at all. Lady Amelia Chase was not interesting enough to be the object of gossip. Even after the incident in the Park. The people who did speak of it only mentioned Phoebe Westing. Amelia ought to have been glad, she knew, but she wondered if anyone would even notice when she was gone from London. It made her feel a little like a ghost, lingering but not belonging to the present. Not belonging anywhere.

"My lady," said a deep voice behind her.

She turned, fearing she had been discovered. She faced a fellow harlequin dressed in black and shades of gray, with a deep gray dragon perched on his shoulder and a pool of shadows creeping behind him like supplicants. Drat. Of course, Lord Blackerby would see through her disguise.

But he studied her with interest. Perhaps he had not recognized her after all.

"I feel it is only appropriate we should dance, do you not?" Blackerby asked.

Amelia only nodded, not wanting her voice to give her away. Blackerby guided her out to the dance floor. As it was not Almack's, the waltz was permitted, and Blackerby danced it well. Amelia had danced with him before, but he had not singled her out for the honor recently. She was not usually interesting enough for him.

"Have you been in London long?" Blackerby asked.

She tilted her head in response again.

"Long enough that I would know your voice, you suppose."

She raised an eyebrow at him and said nothing more.

He laughed. "Some might think I had found the ideal woman. Lovely and silent."

He was trying to bait her, but she only smirked at him and trod on his toes.

He took it in stride, however, with only a wicked grin in response to her intentional misstep. "Very well, my dear. I will make my own guesses, then. This is not your first Season, since you are clearly well versed in surviving London. You are clever. Maybe too clever for your own good. Hmm. I am trying to decide, however, if it is the cleverness or the lack of dowry that has kept you single."

Amelia gasped at his rudeness and pulled away.

Blackerby followed. "Come, did I say too much? If you'd like to speak, you can give me back worse. Somehow, I think you are capable of it."

She was, and she did not need to prove it to him or anyone else. She managed to dodge away from him and get lost in the crowd. Working her way to the edge of the room, she was so focused on avoiding Blackerby that she did not look where she was going. She almost collided with a man in a white bauta mask.

The man glanced her way, though she could not read his expression behind the mask. Her heart hammered, and she pivoted to walk the other direction, forcing herself not to look back. Bauta masks were not unheard of at costume balls. It was probably not the man who had aimed a pistol at her heart. And even if it were—which it was not—he would not recognize her.

Still, the room had become too hot. Too crowded. Amelia's mask clung to her face, making her itch, and she felt light-headed.

Slipping out of the ballroom, Amelia found her way into the library to catch her breath. She started to untie her mask, but she heard voices coming doing the corridor toward her. She did not want to get caught in the midst of a lover's tryst. Thanks to many hours spent in the house with Millicent, she knew of a servant's entrance to the room, so she opened the hidden door and slipped inside, leaving it cracked just enough that she didn't feel trapped in the dark.

"Empty," said one man.

"For the moment," said another.

Amelia raised her eyebrows. Not a lover's tryst. Or, a very scandalous one. She ignored the righteous promptings of whatever angel might be hovering over her shoulder and leaned closer to listen.

"Tell me what you found." This voice sounded pompous. Aristocratic.

"The Prince Regent will be attending a ball next week. We should be able to catch him there." The other man had a rougher accent.

"Excellent. He cannot avoid us forever."

Amelia rolled her eyes. It sounded like nothing more than politics.

The door creaked, and a female voice said. "Oh! I must have taken a wrong turn. Excuse me."

The men muttered their own apologies.

Amelia glanced through the crack to see the embarrassed-looking young lady facing off with the men. Their backs were to Amelia, but from their postures, they also felt awkward. One of them reached out a hand, perhaps in a gesture of apology. Amelia stifled a laugh. The library was too popular a place for trysts of whatever type. She would have to remember that. Not that she was ever likely to have a tryst.

The sound of the girl's light footsteps retreated, and the men murmured a few words to each other and left as well.

Seeing her opportunity, Amelia stepped out and went to sit on the sofa, snatching a book of poetry from the shelf.

In a few minutes, a man in a domino mask peered into the room, his expression hopeful. He gave a start when he saw Amelia.

"Looking for something to read?" she asked.

"Err." He looked at the bookshelves. "I believe I took a wrong turn."

He hurried away, and Amelia chuckled to herself. There went the young lady's match. She did hope the lovers were able to find each other again. But since their tryst was already ruined, she thought she could gain some amusement out of the situation.

The poems about the court of Charlemagne caught her fancy, and she settled in to read, enjoying the magical and melodramatic adventures of the French knights and ladies. Perhaps Miss Charity would branch out from King Arthur's court to include some of these colorful characters. Until that happened, Amelia would have to borrow the book and return it to Millicent later. She stood to go, and Lord Blackerby strode into the room.

They stared at each other for a moment.

"Meeting someone here?" he asked, an eyebrow raised.

She smirked at him and moved to go past. He stood as if he would block her exit, his eyes suspicious. His dragon hopped down and trotted over to sniff at her skirts. She stepped back. After a long moment, Blackerby stepped closer.

"Come, trickster. Maybe your games are not all innocent. There's trouble afoot tonight. I think it's time we do have a talk."

Amelia clutched the book and backed toward the secret door. She didn't like the way he looked at her. Shadows slithered along the floor, reaching for her. Had she interfered with some scheme of Blackerby's? Something with the two men? Or with the man or the girl? The man in the white bauta mask? With Blackerby around, Amelia didn't know if anything was what it seemed. She was not sure she could trust the earl.

She yanked the servant's door open and darted through, slamming it shut behind her so that the latch clicked into place. That would only buy her a moment. She dropped the book and raced down the dim, narrow corridor, stripping off her jester's cap and the outer layer of her old-fashioned dress and tossing them behind her.

Voices and the racket of clinking glasses reached her, and she bounded into the confusion of servants bringing food and drink into the party.

She caught one of the serving girls who was about her size and pulled the young lady into an unused drawing room.

"I'll buy your dress from you," Amelia said.

"What?" the girl asked, clearly thinking this member of the gentry had finally lost her mind.

"I need a new dress. You can have mine, plus two shillings."

The girl's eyes widened. "All right, then, miss."

They quickly swapped clothes. Amelia made sure her mask still covered her eyes then rushed back to the ballroom to push her way into the crowds. She hoped in the dark, her most obvious feature—the red, red hair—would have slipped the girl's notice, and Blackerby would be left with nothing but some discarded clothing to make him wonder who she was and what she might know.

"Amelia!" Lady Millicent said, taking her arm. "What a fantastic costume. A peasant girl? I almost didn't recognize you."

Amelia smiled weakly. She would have to come up with a good story for her mother about why she had changed clothes, but that seemed less threatening than dealing with Lord Blackerby. She'd had enough of secrets for one night.

Chapter Four

SEVERAL WEEKS PASSED QUIETLY, and Amelia began to hope her escapade at the costume ball had gone unnoticed, or at least unconnected to her. She felt silly for having been so out of sorts with Lord Blackerby, but the man was infuriating: arrogant, relentless, and a little too observant.

At least Amelia didn't have to worry about coming across Lord Blackerby and accidentally revealing herself as the jester at the costume ball. Between the incident in Hyde Park and her mother's shock at Amelia's story of trading costumes with another lady at the ball to quiz their friends, her parents kept her under strict surveillance. She was allowed one card party and one dinner party with her mother where she sat very quietly and listened to gossip without contributing to it. She itched to check the post at the Cheapside coffee shop where she had her clandestine correspondence directed, but her mother was not allowing any shopping excursions—especially not to Cheapside.

Amelia sat working on a sketch of the little street sweep who frequented Grosvenor Square, while her mother opened the post. It was a foggy morning, with all the world gray and indistinct. Amelia glanced at the listless figure in her sketch and compared it to the rather more energetic face of her subject and realized she was in danger of falling into a blue study. She had to stop brooding.

Her mother sighed the kind of sigh that was meant to be overheard.

"What is it, Mother?" Amelia asked, setting her charcoal and paper aside.

"Oh, your cousin in Fleet Street. She is feeling neglected."

The cousin, Mrs. Jonston, a young widow living on very restricted means, *was* neglected by her family, but she was not usually one to complain of it. "Does she say as much?"

"Oh, no. But she writes that she hopes we are well and that it has been so very long since she's seen us."

"Are we to visit her, then?" Amelia asked, trying not to sound hopeful. Not only did she like her cousin, but the woman lived conveniently close to the coffee shop where Amelia's letters no doubt waited for her attention.

"I dislike going out in such damp, disagreeable conditions," her mother said, twisting the letter and frowning at the fog outside. "It brings on my cough." She cleared her throat for good measure.

"I would not mind making such a charitable visit," Amelia said. When her mother gave her a skeptical look, she added, "I would take Jane, of course."

With neither husband, advanced age, nor dragon to protect her person or reputation, Amelia often took her maid on trips around London. Jane was good natured and easily distracted by the baubles in shop windows, which made her an ideal companion.

Her mother sighed again and studied the letter. "I suppose it is our duty to family. I ought to go as well—" She cleared her throat again. "But this weather."

"Of course. I will convey your respects."

"You will hire a hackney coach. An inexpensive one."

"Yes, Mother." There were always several near Grosvenor Street, hoping to pick up members of Society with flush pockets.

Amelia went to fetch her bonnet and inform Jane of their plans. The girl was mending sheets and looked extremely grateful to put the tedious task aside. Eventually, Amelia reflected, the sheets would be more stitching than linen, but her father felt no need to replace them. He simply never invited company to spend the night, so no one need know about their little economies.

"What shops are we going to visit?" Jane asked as they walked onto the front steps. The girl practically bounced on her toes at the opportunity to escape the house, despite the wet, sooty stink of the fog rolling in like some primordial beast creeping from the Thames to stalk them. Jane waved her hand. "It feels rather close today, doesn't it? If only there was a breeze."

"Yes. Perhaps we will want fans." Amelia turned back for the door.

A sharp crack made her jump. Something whined as it sailed past her ear and slammed into the door, and a neat, round hole appeared in the wood. An echo bounced off the neighboring houses until the fog swallowed it.

Amelia stared at the hole in abstract fascination. She was not very familiar with guns, but this appeared to be a bullet hole. If her head had been in a slightly different location, that hole might have been in her skull instead.

"How fortunate," she said to no one in particular.

"What was that?" Jane's voice was tight and edged with hysteria. "Was that a gunshot? Oh, look!"

The maid raised a trembling hand to point across the square, where a male figure fled through the fog. The few people who were out stared after him, and one quick-thinking gentleman took off in pursuit, though Amelia thought the fleeing man had too great a head start. She had a strong sense that the man wore a white bauta mask. Her fingers trembled, but she balled them into fists.

"Yes," Amelia said slowly. "I do believe that was a gunshot. But he missed."

The maid turned to see the hole in the door. Her eyes widened. "He almost *hit* us?" Her gaze went vacant. "He almost hit us. Hit *us*."

Jane might have been working up to a fit of hysteria or a swoon, but Amelia didn't have the time for either, so she grabbed the girl's shoulders, gave her a gentle shake, and lied. "I'm sure it was only an accident."

The bullet that had gone through the door might have hit someone on the other side, though, so Amelia left the pale girl to sink onto the stone steps and threw the door open.

The butler, Moore, stood over a shattered vase—the one Lady Hayes used for flower arrangements—looking perplexed.

"Moore?" Amelia asked. "Was anyone hurt?"

"Hurt? No, my lady, this vase just exploded for no reason. I wonder if it was magic. Water magic, perhaps. But why?"

Amelia pointed to the wall, where the lead bullet winked dully from the white plaster. "Not magic."

"A bullet!" he cried, looking torn between fear and outrage. "Is this what we've come to? People shooting off guns in the square?"

"At least no one was injured."

"No. No. Only the vase."

"Yes. Father will be unhappy about that." Amelia wouldn't miss it —her mother had bought it to display flowers sent to Amelia her first Season, and it had stood empty until her mother decided to fill it herself. "At least this will be easier to clean up than blood."

At that, Moore went pale, and Amelia was afraid she was going to lose him. Where did her mother keep her smelling salts? Amelia suspected she would need them for someone before the day was over.

"Moore," she said sharply to keep his attention. "I need you to go to the end of the corridor and make certain no one else comes in here. I'm sure at any moment—"

Someone pounded on the door.

She sighed. "Yes, here they are. Moore, I will talk to them. You guard the corridor. You understand?"

"Yes, my lady." The usually unflappable Moore went as meekly as a kitten to watch the corridor.

Amelia answered the door herself. The constable standing there—a fellow redhead, she noted—looked surprised to have a lady of the house answer his knock. Jane hung on his arm, her eyes watery.

Amelia guided Jane into the house, directing her to go lie down, and turned to the constable. "I suppose you have some questions?"

"Er, that I do, miss. I take it there was an accident with a firearm here?"

"A bullet came through the door." She opened the door wider to show him. "Fortunately, the only casualty was that vase, which I believe was a reproduction."

He glanced into the entrance hall. "May I?"

"Yes, please come see."

She shut the door on the crowd gathered to see what the excitement was about. The big red-headed man—whom Amelia vaguely recognized as a Bow Street Runner who had worked with the Westings in the past, and not the normal beat constable—studied the bullet in the wall, then carefully pried it out. He glanced back at her.

"I understand there was a lady outside when the shot was fired," he said.

"Yes, that was I."

"Did you see who fired the shot?"

"No, my face was turned away. My maid, whom you were kind enough to help inside, did spot someone running away. A man—that's all I can be sure of. She might be able to tell you more."

"I did take a statement from her." His expression said it had been more hysterical than helpful.

"I imagine there must be a dozen witnesses from around the square."

"Ah, well, in the fog and the confusion..." the man rubbed the back of his neck.

"There are also a dozen different stories?"

He smiled ruefully. "You've got the right of it, miss." He looked around at the mess. "I don't think we need anything else here. Your people can clean up."

There was a squawk from Moore at the far end of the corridor.

A mocking male voice said, "there's at least one more thing we need."

The Earl of Blackerby. Sneaking about in her house.

Amelia pursed her lips and turned to face the earl, who stood at the end of the corridor, a dragon perched on his shoulder, and mists of darkness trailing behind him. Always so dramatic.

"You could not just come in through the front door, my lord?" she asked.

He smirked. "I might have missed a clue. And I certainly would have missed that look of surprise on your face. It lends such a lovely blush to your cheeks."

The annoyance burning across her face, Amelia knew, was much darker than a delicate blush. Drat her red-headed complexion. "And did you find any clues by sneaking in through the kitchen?"

"Only that your cook is preparing a delicious-looking supper."

"You will not be invited to stay."

"Such a generous hostess," Blackerby said, his eyes dancing with amusement. "It's so surprising anyone would take a shot at you."

The Bow Street Runner gaped at Blackerby, his master, but Amelia only glared.

Of course, Blackerby was right. Both that the bullet had likely been meant for her—a part of her had registered that immediately and pushed it aside—and also, that she was not particularly well-liked. She had never had that ease with people that made conversation flow naturally, so although she did not, in general, dislike people, she often found herself at arm's length from them. She knew many thought her rude or at least snobbish, but she did not know how to alter their opinion of her, so she let it stand. Still, until the past month, she had gone nearly twenty-one years without offending someone so badly that they felt the need to shoot at her.

"I believe you are done here, my lord." She said the last words with as much bite as she could muster.

He only smiled. "Parting is such sweet sorrow." He turned to the Runner. "Did you get everything you needed, Farris?"

"Aye, my lord. I have the bullet, and I've talked to such witnesses as there were."

"And what conclusions have you drawn?"

The Runner, Farris, glanced at Amelia and licked his lips nervously. "I still would like to investigate more…"

"Never fear, Farris. Lady Amelia is made of stern stuff. You agree with me that someone shot at her?"

"I'm afraid so, my lord." Farris looked apologetically at Amelia.

Blackerby strode so close to Amelia that the sandalwood and cinnamon aroma of his *eau de cologne* drifted around her. He had worn the same scent at the costume ball. His brown eyes fixed hers. "I did say there was one more thing that I needed. Can you think of any reason at all that someone might want to shoot at you? Any scandals or secrets you wish to divulge?" He leaned closer. "I am excellent at keeping confidences."

The intimate, almost seductive tone of his voice sent a not-unpleasant shiver through her.

Amelia drew a sharp breath and stepped back to open the door for him. Then she lied to his face. "None at all, my lord. Good day."

Farris bowed and hurried out. Blackerby lingered for a moment, watching Amelia curiously. She kept her chin high and refused to flinch from his scrutiny. His gaze darted to his dragon, who was lurking around Amelia's hems. The earl made a clicking noise, and the dragon hopped onto his shoulder. He smirked and bowed deeply.

"Until next time, my lady," he said, tipping his hat as he exited.

She shut the door firmly behind him, her heart beating too fast. Just from the shock of being shot at, she told herself. But she never could lie to herself.

Maybe London really didn't agree with her. Maybe it was time to accept that she was on the shelf and retire to the country. There, she would be away from deep voices trying to slither secrets out of her. There, people shot at the pheasants and not the ladies.

Blackerby practically skipped down Grosvenor Street, forcing Farris to hurry to keep up. He swung his walking stick as he went, energized by the mysteries and secrets churning in the fog.

"What do you think?" Blackerby asked, glancing back at his loyal Runner.

Farris eyed him warily. Blackerby liked to ask vague questions—it told him so much more, not only about the situation, but about the thought process of his subordinates—but Farris had worked for him for several years and grown canny to his ways.

"I think Lady Amelia is an interesting woman, sir."

"Oh, do you?" Blackerby smiled, trying to decipher which way Farris's mind was turning. The Runner liked women, as far as Blackerby could tell, but his head wasn't often turned by them. Even one as admittedly fascinating as Lady Amelia.

"It isn't every woman who holds her own against you, my lord."

Blackerby raised a hand to his chest. "Holds her own? Do you mean to suggest that I did not have her bested?"

"She lied to you and showed you on your way."

Blackerby chuckled. "You caught the lie, too? Good man. It's strange, though, isn't it? What does she have to hide? It's rare for anyone to take shots at ladies. And since we exclude the fairer sex from politics and war, it is love that's most likely to kill them. Especially the upper-class ones. Lady Amelia is not a serious player in Society, yet she is neither dragon-linked nor anti-magic. An affair of the heart seems the most likely cause for such vitriol."

"Too true," Farris said glumly.

Uh-oh. Blackerby gave him a keener look. Farris sounded like he was taking the topic to heart. The idea of Farris infatuated with Lady Amelia bothered Blackerby, though he couldn't say why. Probably simply because it was so inconvenient to have one of his Runners entangled.

"Have you taken a liking to Lady Amelia?" Blackerby asked.

"Me?" Farris looked sincerely taken aback. "A lady like her? No, sir. Why?"

Blackerby pretended nonchalance. "Oh, because someone is going to have to spy on Lady Amelia and find out her secret. If she does have some troublesome lover taking shots at her, we need to put a stop to it. Sets a bad precedence."

Farris grunted a grudging agreement.

When they reached Bond Street, Blackerby dismissed the Runner—for the moment—and continued to his offices in Whitehall. The fog near the river was especially thick, hiding the towers of Westminster and anyone bold enough to stroll in St. James's with the pickpockets out in force. The streets felt close and dark, and Blackerby felt at home, his steps never faltering in the dusky light.

Blackerby climbed the stairs to his offices and shooed Shade off his shoulder, then settled into a chair and propped his feet on his desk. He picked up the knife he used to pry the wax seals off letters and began flipping it, catching it by the handle each time it came down.

Lady Amelia was one problem he needed to solve—or more like a puzzle to unravel. A lover's spat was the only reason he could fathom for someone to shoot at her, but he had never heard of her being romantically entangled with any member of the *haut ton*. Maybe it was with someone beneath her station. She seemed like the type who would attract a rather intense man. There was something about her. Soft, pleasant curves on the outside, but a steely core within. There was potential for passion there. Blackerby contemplated Lady Amelia with her fiery hair and fiery eyes for a moment. Then he shook his head and turned to the dispatches on his desk.

Shaw was Blackerby's real problem. The dragon expert who hated dragons so much that he was determined to purge them from England just as the revolutionaries attempted to do in France. And Shaw might have the key to doing so after the water dragon incident in Lyme Regis had alerted them all to the fact that dragons could be killed.

But Blackerby had no idea where Shaw was or where he would strike, nor did any of his contacts. He was bleeding his personal coffers dry buying every bit of information down to the merest whisper about Shaw, but he had nothing. If only the man moved in Society, there would be plenty of gossip for Blackerby to sift through. Blackerby had hoped the masquerade ball would turn something up, but he was grasping at straws. And meanwhile, Shaw had some way of getting information about the *haut ton*.

"Blast!" Blackerby announced to Shade, who blinked sleepily at him. "He wouldn't be a step ahead of me if he didn't have his spies among us. How do I flush them out?"

Shade yawned.

"Very helpful!" Blackerby huffed.

He threw the dagger, sticking it into the wall, and plopped down on his favorite chair to shuffle through the newspapers. The latest installment of Miss Charity's novel sat in the pile. As good as any gossip column if he sifted through the characters' identities. Some were easier than others. He picked the book up and flipped through it. Knights and ladies, princes and monsters, all thinly disguised members of Society. He personally liked his own jester character. Miss Charity had a soft spot for him, he thought. Whomever she was. He had considered tracking her down, but she continued to prove both entertaining and useful, so he didn't interfere.

A scene in the story made him stop, though. It sounded familiar. Too familiar. A couple dancing at a masquerade, the lady poor but good and clever, the man an oafish buffoon.

"You might be married if you had less wit and more money," the bumbling man said.

The lady stomped on the man's foot and left in a huff.

Blackerby leaned forward as if trying to see behind the words printed on the page. "Well, Miss Charity, you are a trickster after all! And I suppose I am no longer a favorite of yours."

Shade blinked sleepily and looked up at him.

"You see," Blackerby said to his companion, "That scene is a little too close to the one I had with the harlequin at the costume ball. With Miss Charity, it would seem. What a clever way to gather material for her books. So, perhaps it was a publisher she was meeting in the library. Or was it? Hmm."

He frowned and thumbed over the edge of the book. He had always considered Miss Charity harmless, but now he wondered. He had heard whisperings that a group of ne'er-do-wells had planned to meet at Lady Millicent's costume ball. Miss Charity could be one of them. She—Or he? No, that figure had looked genuinely feminine— moved in Society yet was clearly critical of her peers. She could be discontented enough to pass on information to the Luddites through the Miss Charity books. It would be clever, acting right under everyone's noses.

And he had ignored her all this time. He stood, raising the book to fling it aside, then recollected himself and opened it to find the publisher's address. He had to track down Miss Charity, though she was probably wise enough to cover her tracks. He strode to his desk and pulled the lady's discarded harlequin hat from his drawer, running his fingers once again over the smooth green-and-purple silk, the neat stitches made by a careful hand. He didn't know what had impelled him to keep it, but now he suspected it had been instinct. He and the mysterious lady would finally have that chat.

Chapter Five

AMELIA SAT at the desk in the library, tapping her pen on her lower lip. Her publisher's last letter had demanded the next installment of Miss Charity's work immediately, but she had put the Black Knight into quite a fix, and she wasn't sure how to get him out of it. Perhaps Lord Jasper's character could ride to the rescue. Amelia was much more pleased with how he was treating his wife of late. He could have a heroic moment.

"There's no need to announce me," came Lady Millicent's voice. "Darling Amelia is always at home to me."

Amelia gave a start and shoved her writing under some books then stood to welcome her old friend. Millicent floated into the room, pushing past the butler, who gave Amelia an apologetic look.

Millicent shut the door and her dragon hopped down from her shoulder. "Amelia! I'm so glad to find you at home. I cannot bear to listen to Mother another moment."

She threw herself down on the chair in a pose of despair. Her dragon jumped to her lap and rubbed its head against her chin consolingly. Amelia couldn't help smiling at her theatrics. She sat next to Millicent and patted her hand.

"Tell me all."

"She says I must marry. Of course, I don't mind the idea in theory —I was quite ready to be Lady Westing, you know, with either of the brothers—but now there is no one suitable. It seems that the old families are failing. It is too bad your brother is already married. I don't suppose his wife is sickly?"

Amelia's mouth twitched, but she managed not to laugh at Millicent's abominable rudeness. "No, she is quite healthy. Safely delivered of two children."

Millicent sighed. Amelia refrained from mentioning that her very sturdy and serious older brother would not find Millicent's strong personality comfortable.

"You've had several offers since the elder Westing," Amelia said.

"Oh, a few. But none that Father would give his approval to. Darling Pierre Moreau simply dotes on me, and I am quite smitten with him, but he is French. The one time Father went to Paris before the Revolution, it rained on him the whole time, and he has taken a loathing to the entire race in consequence. And there is Mr. Hastings. He is jolly enough. Not bad looking, very gentlemanly, but he has that cousin who is a solicitor. Not that I would hold it against him—we cannot help our cousins, after all—but Father dislikes lawyers excessively."

"It is a shame your father is so broad in his dislikes."

"Oh, he is a cranky old thing, but we do have royal blood, after all, so I suppose he has a right to expect something worthy of us." Her eyes brightened. "You ought to marry my brother! Father might complain less then. You would be acceptable, at least."

"I don't think your brother and I would suit," Amelia said. Which was putting it delicately. She disliked the boorish Randolph Blanchfield as much as their father disliked the French and lawyers all put together. "Doesn't he wish to marry someone dragon linked? He seemed quite interested in Eliza Prescott."

Millicent huffed and waved a hand. "I think that was only to bother our parents. They would have been outraged to have a connection who wasn't from one of the best families. Father would disinherit my brother if he could, but since titles must go to the eldest son, my brother does everything he can to provoke our parents. Father will try to live forever just to spite him."

Amelia laughed at that. "I'm sorry about your father, dear. Our parents are quite a bother, are they not?" Her parents reminded her that she was never good enough, and Millicent's family thought they were too good for everyone. She wasn't sure which was worse.

Millicent sighed. "What are you going to do about yours?"

Amelia's gaze darted to where her writing papers lay hidden, but she quickly looked back at Millicent. "I may become a companion for one of my elderly cousins. I have so many of them, you know."

"A companion." Millicent wrinkled her nose.

"I would not mind it so much. My elderly relations are sweet, eccentric creatures, and not very demanding. I could pursue other interests while they napped, and if they tell me the same stories over and over again, well, at least I won't have to pay much attention."

She could continue writing and they wouldn't be the wiser. Maybe she could even try her hand at something more serious than parodies of her peers. It had been amusing to start out with, a way to strike back against her parents and the Society that mostly scorned her, and which she scorned in return. But she had been surprised to find, not only that people wanted to read what she wrote, but also that she enjoyed doing it. She wondered if she wrote seriously if she might be able to support herself.

"I cannot picture you locked away like that," Millicent said.

Amelia's chest tightened at the thought of being cast off and forgotten in some country estate, but she shook her head. It was not so different from being forgotten right there in London, and it was possibly more lonely to feel isolated surrounded by people than in the peace of the countryside. "You cannot picture yourself being locked away. I confess I would miss the bustle of London, but I would hardly be a prisoner, and I would escape from Father's sour moods."

Millicent gave her a sympathetic look, but before she could say anything, the butler tapped at the door.

"Enter," Amelia said.

"Apologies, my lady. He was insistent." Moore held out a tray with a visiting card. Amelia raised an eyebrow. She was unusually popular that day. She lifted the card and almost dropped it when she saw the name printed on it in looping calligraphy. The Earl of Blackerby.

"Oh, what can he want?" Amelia muttered.

Millicent raised both eyebrows. "Him?" She glanced at the card, and a cunning look entered her eyes. "Does he call on you often?"

"No. At least, he usually calls on Father."

"To be the Countess of Blackerby might not be entirely bad."

"I have no desire to marry a flirt and a...a lunatic," Amelia said. "But I'm sure that's not why he is calling." A cold, wormy feeling in her stomach warned her that she had been caught. Though why or how she did not know.

"Well," Millicent said. "Regardless of why he has come, I think I will leave you alone with him for this tête-à-tête."

"That's not necessary!" Amelia said.

But Millicent gave her a coy smile and stepped out of the room. Amelia growled at her friend's back, then composed herself to face Lord Blackerby.

"Show him in," she told Moore.

The shadows preceded him. Amelia rolled her eyes. She didn't know much about how magic worked, but she suspected he did that on purpose. Men often complained that women were dramatic, but no one could outperform the Earl of Blackerby.

He strode into the room, his expression, as always, a little sardonic and otherwise difficult to read. He was handsome in a devilish sort of way, with his sharply defined cheekbones and unruly dark hair. It was all calculated to make him interesting, she was certain. It worked, at least a little, as she always wondered what he was thinking.

"Good day, my lord," Amelia said. "You wished to see me? Should I call for a chaperone?"

He smirked. "No, that won't be necessary. I have not come to make love to you. I am here on business."

Amelia's eyes narrowed at the insinuation that she was below his notice as a woman, but she was well schooled and did not otherwise express her annoyance. "Very well. Take a seat, please."

Of course, he did not, choosing instead to pace his way around the room, pretending to examine the books. Like a tiger in a cage at the Royal Menagerie. "I saw Lady Millicent leave."

"Yes." Amelia wasn't sure what else to say to that.

"Did you enjoy her masquerade ball?"

So, that was it. Amelia should have guessed he would discover her identity eventually. But other than treading on his foot, she had done nothing wrong. And she did not regret that action in the least. She was tempted to do it again. But she would not admit so quickly to her wrongdoing.

She tilted her head. "I did, my lord. Were you in attendance?"

He quirked one eyebrow. "Ah, are we playing games?"

"Aren't we always?" she asked as his dragon came up to sniff at the little hole in her worn-out slipper. She had been meaning to mend that.

Blackerby, like a magician in a street show, pulled from under his finely tailored coat her harlequin hat. "I have been carrying this around like the prince with his slipper, trying to find the lady it fits." He pulled from within the hat a single red hair.

She flushed. Curse her red hair and her easy blush. And curse Blackerby for poking fun at her slipper, which he had surely noticed. She pursed her lips. "You have promoted yourself to prince now?"

He laughed at that, a deep, hearty chuckle. "No, thank you. But you have promoted me to the wise fool, have you not?"

"You are the one carrying the jester's cap, my lord."

"And you, my lady, seem to think it belongs on my head."

"Your attire is not my concern. I am not your valet."

He bowed his head in acknowledgment. "My valet is not a very witty fellow, though he knows how to stay out of one's way when one wants it. You, I think, have a different problem. You have a sharp tongue and an even sharper pen, and you want to be in the way."

"I don't wish to be in anyone's way."

"Don't you?" Blackerby asked.

Amelia narrowed her eyes. "Of what are you accusing me, my lord?"

"Of being witty. Do you take exception to that?"

"I do. A lady is charming, not witty."

Blackerby's eyes flashed as though he had come upon some

revelation. "Of course! That's why you do it. I admit I had not suspected you. Your disguise is excellent. But I think, secretly, perhaps you wanted to be caught so your wit could be known."

Amelia stood. She was still much shorter than Blackerby, but at least she felt at less of a disadvantage. "Speak plainly, my lord. You take shots at me from around corners."

"Not I." His gaze swept the room, and he smiled. His dragon had hopped onto the desk. Blackerby strode over and pulled Miss Charity's papers from their hiding place. "But I believe someone wants Miss Charity dead."

Amelia drew a sharp breath, but it was hard to deny it while he held the proof in his hands. How had he discovered her? Not even her publisher knew her identity. "Those belong to my lady's maid. She writes to amuse herself."

"Hmm. A clever explanation. But your lady's maid did not tread upon my toes at the masquerade."

Amelia went cold at that. She had not disguised the scene well enough, then. And the red hair in the jester's hat had betrayed her. But she stayed her course. "I tell my maid everything."

"I doubt that. You keep your councils, Lady Amelia. I have watched you closely. Watching clever people is one of my duties. And even if you dress up as one, you are no fool. I suppose you're going to tell me you allowed your lady's maid to run off to the ball in disguise?"

Amelia wished she had tried that tack. Though, of course, Blackerby would eventually want to talk to Jane, who certainly would not fool him. "You read too many fairy stories, my lord. It would be disrespectful to allow her to attend Millicent's party."

"But not disrespectful to allow her to insult your peers? Come, Lady Amelia. I am not the only one to have discovered your identity. Because someone is trying to kill you. Or, rather, to silence Miss Charity. We can discuss the matter here, in private, or I can bring you down to my offices and make a spectacle of it. I do not think Society will be kind to you when they know it is you who have lampooned them."

Amelia felt the blood drain from her cheeks. "You would not be so crass as to violate a lady's privacy and expose her to scorn."

"As you have exposed so many? You should never do anything you would be ashamed to own later, Lady Amelia. Secrets want to be told, and they find their way to the light."

That was what Amelia had always feared and never allowed herself to consider. She glared and sank into a chair. "I don't think Miss Charity has insulted anyone seriously enough to provoke them to murder."

"Ah, but maybe a fellow spy has turned on her? Traitors have a tendency to do that, you know."

Amelia gave him a confused look. "Now you truly are weaving fairy stories. What on earth are you talking about?"

Blackerby tossed the hat into her lap. "Who were you meeting in the library at the masquerade? How did you disappear so thoroughly?"

Amelia stared at him for a long moment, and a smile slowly spread over face. She laughed. Blackerby looked so put out, that she laughed even harder, until tears streamed from the corners of her eyes.

She wiped her cheeks dry. "Forgive me, my lord, but you must see wickedness everywhere. I find parties tiring, especially when I'm forced to dance with arrogant earls, and I was in the library to read."

He studied her, his eyes glinting with suspicion. "And the secret doorway?"

"I have known the Blanchfields since we were children. There's not a servant's passage or a priests hole anywhere in either of their houses that I don't know about."

"Why run if you were not guilty? Why hide your voice?"

"You had insulted me, my lord. I had no interest in revealing myself to you."

He stared for a long moment, perhaps trying to recall that night. He probably threw out insults so often he wasn't even aware he was doing it. "I see. I did not think you the missish sort."

Amelia curled her lip up. "It is not being missish to expect to be treated with some respect. I am the daughter of a Marquess. You are tossing out insults to cover your own bad behavior. And though I don't like to admit it, my father might be right in this instance. Perhaps you could stand to be reminded of how an earl ought to behave."

Blackerby raised both eyebrows at that. "Well, well. The fox has teeth. I can see Miss Charity could bite harder if she wished."

"Hang Miss Charity!"

"Someone would like to. If I take you at your word that you are not a spy, why would Miss Charity's tales elicit such a strong reaction from someone?"

She rubbed her forehead. "Perhaps they simply don't like being insulted. Few people do."

"If that were the case, why not expose you? That would put an end to your literary career."

It certainly would. She really would have to go live in the country, a dishonored woman. Her opportunities to write something serious would probably be lost forever. Despite what Blackerby thought, she did not want to be caught.

"Yes," Blackerby said. "I think you see. So, why would someone want to silence Miss Charity without revealing her?"

"Maybe someone just doesn't like redheads."

"It seems a bit extreme."

He studied her like he was considering her. Like he could see into her. Amelia had heard enough rumors about Blackerby's abilities to wonder if that was possible.

Finally, he said, "Lady Amelia, did you see anyone else at the library that night?"

"Well, yes." She told him about the two men and the interrupted tryst between the lady and the gentleman.

"Did you see any of them? Did they see you?"

"I was hiding in the servant's passage, so they did not see me. I saw the woman through the crack, however, and I met her lover. I had come out and was reading my book by then. He looked quite embarrassed and hurried away."

"Did you recognize him?"

"In fact, I didn't. But I don't know everyone in the *haut ton*."

"Hmm."

"Oh, you really suspect the unfortunate man whose lady I scared away could be a danger to anyone? Don't you believe in love?"

"I distrust it. For now, the two gentlemen interest me more. You said they mentioned Prinny?"

"Yes, though they were more formal. Called him the Prince Regent. I assumed they had some political agenda."

"Well, assassination is very political."

Amelia paled. "Surely, it couldn't be that serious."

"You were in Dorset during the water dragon incident. You know how serious these Luddites are. If they were able to assassinate Prinny, with the king still mad after his dragon was poisoned, the country would be thrown into chaos."

"Why are you so certain it's the Luddites?"

"Because my spies informed me that miscreants would be meeting at the masquerade ball, and now I hear rumors that the Luddites are planning something—something big—for this week."

"But Luddites would not care for me."

"You really are contrary, my lady. Are you certain they did not see you? Or somehow connect you to the library? If they knew you had overheard them, you would be in great danger. It would explain the shot fired at you."

"I…" She thought about the second gentleman who had come into the library. And the servants who had seen her in the passageway. "I cannot guarantee that they couldn't make the connection. You did, after all. Oh, but the gunshot wasn't the first time someone tried to kill me."

"Not the… Hyde Park. Yes. We cannot connect the two for certain, but I dislike coincidences."

"As do I, especially when they involve people trying to kill me."

"If not the masquerade ball, then why such violent dislike of you? Do you have any scorned lovers pining for you?"

"None at all," Amelia said, struggling to keep a bitter note out of her words.

"We could fall back on the theory that there is someone with a vendetta against redheads, but I don't trust the Luddites enough to leave them out of consideration. Perhaps Miss Charity has raised their ire somehow."

"I'm not sure what I could possibly have to do with them, but I would like to see them stopped."

Blackerby looked thoughtful for a few moments. "Perhaps you can help. We don't know for certain why you are being targeted, but you overheard the men in the library. We will attend the ball with Prinny and see if you can identify the voices of the men you heard scheming against him."

"So, there are people who may be trying to silence me, and you want to take me to a party with them?"

He grinned. "Yes, you've grasped it exactly. Once their plot is uncovered, you should be out of danger. Unless, of course, your attacker is simply an anti-red-head maniac."

Amelia stared at him, trying to decide if he was serious. She had a feeling that, with Blackerby around, she was far from being out of danger.

Chapter Six

AMELIA HAD NOT EXPECTED any trouble from her mother regarding the party, but Lady Hayes' face paled when Amelia asked about it at supper.

"A party with the Prince Regent?" Her mother dabbed her face with her napkin. "Oh, I do not think that would be wise."

"I'm certain there is no danger, Mother."

"And I am certain there is. No, we cannot risk it."

It warmed Amelia to think that her mother cared for her safety after all, but she did not want to see the Prince Regent harmed if she could stop it, and she did not trust what Blackerby might do with her secret if she didn't help.

Amelia poked at the crab leg on her plate, thinking of the best way around her mother. "There will be ever so many fashionable people there. Not the sort of place one is likely to see firearms."

Unless they were bringing them for the Prince Regent.

"Firearms?" Lady Hayes exclaimed, setting aside her glass. "What are you babbling about, child?"

Amelia wrinkled her forehead. "Your fear that someone might shoot at me."

"Don't be ridiculous. That was simply an accident. No, my fear is that we do not have gowns fine enough for such an occasion."

Amelia lay her fork down with a heavy thunk. Of course, fashion was her mother's concern. She was tempted to point out that the Prince Regent was no Bond Street Beau himself, not quite able to keep up with London's most fashionable set. But that would not help her case.

Her father cleared his throat. "There will be eligible men at this event, I presume?"

"Naturally," Amelia said, surprised to find help from such an unlikely quarter.

Lord Hayes looked to his wife. "You'd better take her, then. Do your best with whatever gowns you have but see if you can get some lord to take notice of her. I rather despair of her, but our family needs a good match, not another spinster draining family resources. In fact, at this point, I would be happy with any match—even an untitled one."

Her mother's eyes brightened. "It might be worth the investment, then, in some new ribbon?"

"If it comes out of your pin money."

Lady Hayes frowned at that.

Fortunately, neither of them paid any heed to Amelia, who bowed her head over her plate as she struggled to control the hot flush brightening her cheeks. She was not going to cry. Not going to show how the discussion humiliated her. This was why she had her books. Someday, they might buy her freedom. Not a respectable place in Society. She had already failed to measure up there. But a small, independent living where she did not have to hear herself discussed like a kidney pie going stale on the shelf? That would be worth the cost.

Determined to focus on the task at hand, Amelia recruited Jane to help her make over a pair of gowns for the ball, adjusting the necklines and adding some ribbon pilfered from an older gown. Jane sewed with a dreamy smile, probably imagining herself going to such an event and catching the eye of a handsome lord. Amelia envied her the ability to dream. Once one had faced reality and found it less rosy, the dreams lost their brightness.

The morning of the ball, Amelia displayed the gowns for her mother.

Lady Hayes eyed them dubiously. "I had hoped we might look a touch more fashionable." She glanced over her shoulder, as if afraid to find her husband frowning at her. "But they will do. I will order sedan chairs to take us, so we don't spoil them. I only hope no one realizes we wore them to Mrs. Hunter's musicale last Season."

Amelia doubted anyone was keeping track of the fashion choices of two reclusive, high-born ladies. Their names were on the guest list because of their position, not because anyone particularly desired their company.

With the exception, Amelia reminded herself, of Millicent Blanchfield and Phoebe Westing. Two such opposite people, and they certainly disliked each other, but Amelia returned a fondness for both of them. And they were both attuned to light. Maybe there was something to that. Millicent had been more like Phoebe when they were young. Before her parents had poisoned her into thinking she had to hold herself above everyone else.

Lord Blackerby desired her company at the ball. The thought circled her mind, but she reminded it that he only wanted her there to identify the men she had overheard speaking of the Prince Regent.

When Amelia exited the sedan chair at the grand townhouse in St. James Square where the ball was held, she was surprised to see two familiar faces, not among the arriving guests, but in the crowd of servants and attendants. Phoebe Westing's urchin, Brainy Jamie, stood whispering with the street sweep Amelia often spotted in Grosvenor Square. How curious. And, like Blackerby, she did not trust coincidences. What was Lord Blackerby scheming?

Amelia and her mother climbed the stairs to the townhouse decorated with false columns and other classical ornamentation and proceeded up to the ballroom. They were announced on entering the room, but their names did not rouse much interest. Amelia was happy to catch sight of the Westings in the crowd, though not surprised after seeing Brainy Jamie outside. Blackerby must have drawn them into this as well. Studying the crowded room, she also caught sight of the West Indian heiress, Eliza Prescott—No, Eliza Parry, now—along with her water dragon and her captain-husband. Interesting. Blackerby was being cautious and including people who'd had dealings with the Luddites in the past.

Phoebe caught sight of Amelia and gave her a genuine smile. Amelia slipped away from her mother to greet Phoebe.

"Amelia!" Phoebe took her hand and pressed it. "I hope you've been well? After the... the incidents?"

Amelia smiled at Phoebe's delicacy. "I'm quite well. But how are you feeling?" she asked with a glance at Phoebe's growing belly.

Phoebe's cheeks glowed. "Oh, much better now than at the beginning! West wanted me to stay home anyway, but I wanted to be here in case..." Her eyes widened, and she bit her lip uncertainly.

Amelia smiled. "Don't worry; I know what's afoot tonight."

"Oh, I'm so glad!" Phoebe said, her voice low. "I would hate to have to deceive a friend."

Lord Westing edged over and bowed to Amelia as he took his lady's elbow. "I apologize for interrupting your tete-a-tete, but we're needed on the other side of the room."

Amelia nodded and waved farewell to Phoebe. Eliza Parry brushed past her, following the Westings. Eliza ignored Amelia, but her purple water dragon flicked its tongue at her. Amelia stifled a laugh at the impertinent gesture.

Her smile faded, however, as she thought of Phoebe's straightforward honesty. How would Phoebe react if she knew Amelia was Miss Charity?

Millicent would be horrified. She would refuse to speak to Amelia for months. But she would eventually forgive her, Amelia was sure.

Phoebe Westing... Amelia hadn't known her as long, but she sensed that Phoebe would be more hurt than offended at Amelia's deception.

For deception it was. Amelia could not deny that something that had started as a fancy to amuse herself had turned into a subterfuge she was playing against everyone in Society. They probably ought not to forgive her, using her position among them to mock them as she did. Yet, she saw no other path to freedom. She had no dowry, dragon, or natural grace and beauty to attract a husband, and marriage was the only occupation for a lady of her standing. Her father would ship her off to Bedlam before allowing her to be a governess, an occupation Amelia had no inclination for anyway.

So, Amelia put on her polite smile and planned to gather good fodder for Miss Charity's next novel. She found herself scanning the crowd for Lord Blackerby. Only because she was supposed to be helping him root out the conspirators who would destroy the kingdom, though. Amelia considered the Prince Regent an abominable man who treated his poor wife disgracefully, but he represented stability against the Luddites at home and Napoleon abroad.

The Prince Regent stood surrounded by a constellation of admirers and sycophants, his earth-attuned dragon lounging by his feet. Lady Hayes was drawn into the orbit. Prinny's prominent nose was much like his father's, but where the ill king had a weak chin, Prinny's jutted stubbornly. His cravat was tied elaborately, and he wore his shirt points starched and tall so that he could not turn his head. The look did not flatter his large figure, but few were brave enough to tell him that.

At least the mob around him would protect him from a direct assault, but the casualties might be rather high.

Amelia scanned the room again for Blackerby. She sensed more than saw him approach, the shadows around her deepening. Soon, he was standing by her elbow, pretending to listen to the Prince Regent prattle on. It would not seem to anyone else that he paid her the slightest heed, but she could feel his attention pinned on her, like light focused by a quizzing glass. It made her feel a bit flushed.

"Ah, look!" the Prince Regent declared, his beady eyes falling on Blackerby. "Here is my pet villain. Shall I have him show us some tricks with his shadows?"

The crowd shifted and muttered, casting uncomfortable glances between the prince who acted like a fool, and the trickster who acted, if not like a prince, at least like a man in control of the situation. They respected the prince's title, but they feared Blackerby's shadows.

The Prince Regent and Blackerby locked gazes for a long moment, and Blackerby didn't need a quizzing glass to make it clear he was looking down on the prince.

Prinny cleared his throat and glanced away. "Ah, Lady Bathurst. You're looking well tonight."

The crowd visibly relaxed at the change of subject. Amelia risked a glance at Blackerby. He was now ignoring the Prince Regent, his focus on the man's audience, studying each as if he really could see into their thoughts.

Amelia needed to pay attention as well. She focused on voices, on identifying the timbres she had heard in the library. One of the voices had been fairly indistinct, but the other was loud, blustery. Not at all like a gentleman.

And that idea struck her. While she hated to agree with her father, it did seem like most of the upper class would only stand to lose if the Luddites overthrew their social order. Look at the blood that had flowed in France, and now Napoleon reigned over Europe as a warlord, exterminating the dragon-linked and everyone connected to them.

Amelia shuddered in spite of herself and turned away from the Prince Regent's inner circle.

"Lady Amelia?" Blackerby whispered, bending close to her.

His low voice sent an odd thrill through her, and she gave him a warning look. She did not need rumors circulating that she was his latest flirt.

She snapped her fan open and fluttered it in front of her face to disguise their conversation. "I don't think the men we're looking for will be this close to Prinn—the Prince Regent. Not part of his circle. There was something in the one's voice… Not entirely refined. I think we want someone who seems a little out of place."

"Excellent thought. Come, walk with me." He offered an arm.

Amelia hesitated. This was exactly the opposite of what she wanted —instead of blending in and listening to gossip, she would be at the center of it. They did not have to search together.

But her mother had noticed the interaction between her and Blackerby, and she gave Amelia a very pointed look. Amelia sighed in defeat. She would not win in a battle of wills against her mother *and* Lord Blackerby. She surrendered and took the earl's arm.

Blackerby was happy enough to get away from the insipid Prince Regent. He served the country, not Prinny, he reminded himself. His attunement to the dark and shadows might make him a natural villain, but at least he chose to use his abilities for a noble cause. The Luddites thought they wanted darkness and chaos, but only because they did not see into it, know the vast emptiness and despair it contained.

"We could search separately," Lady Amelia whispered to him. "Cover more ground."

He glanced down at her. She was no fainting chit of a girl, but her pale skin, delicately freckled and almost glowing under the candlelight, gave him a sense that she was something delicate that ought to be protected. "I don't want to take the chance of someone trying to kill you again. Third time's the charm, eh?"

"Do you really think someone's going to shoot me in the middle of a ball with the Prince Regent standing right there?"

"I would have bet against them shooting at you in Hyde Park or Grosvenor Square, so I have decided I am not a gambling man."

She snorted. Quietly. Almost delicately.

Almost.

They both grew quiet as Lord and Lady Grenwell walked by. Lord Grenwell nodded to Blackerby and continued on his way. Lady Grenwell had eyes only for her husband, though he scarcely seemed to notice she was there; he was so focused on speaking to the right people and avoiding the ones he thought wrong. Lady Grenwell's gaze dropped, and her pace flagged.

Blackerby did not think he would ignore a woman who looked at him like that. Then again, he wasn't sure adoration would suit him. Too much to live up to.

"Thus dies love," Lady Amelia whispered, more to herself than him —probably composing a line for Miss Charity. "You put your whole heart out at the beginning, but you take it back piece by piece."

Blackerby winced inwardly at the sad accuracy of her statement. Lord Grenwell, in what was probably an effort to do his duty and be worthy to be called husband, was missing the very essence of the role.

Blackerby knew well enough how to avoid that mistake. He would never marry. Any woman who wanted to marry Westminster's shadow master was probably not right in the head. Besides, the very wicked should not pass on their legacy to another generation. His own parents, ecstatic at first to find that their child was dragon-linked, grew frightened of having a child attuned to darkness. He was their first and last offspring. Let his family name die with him.

"Do any voices sound familiar?" he asked Lady Amelia, sotto voce.

She shook her head. "We need to circulate more. Maybe toward the outer edges of the room."

He took the cue and guided her through the crowd. It was easy enough. The way parted before them, as it did wherever he went. He could fancy it was out of respect, but of course that was not the case. He saw the wariness and fear in everyone's eyes as he passed. He did what he always did in response: he smirked, and he bowed and found what amusement he could in the situation.

Lady Amelia was almost as adept at ignoring the curious gazes. There was only a slight tightening by her eyes that showed that it bothered her. She certainly was more dignified than Blackerby, for while he smirked, her face remained completely impassive. Not unkind, just unmoved. He admired her steeliness, but also felt a twinge of sympathy for whatever had occurred in her life that had let her build such an impressive wall. Probably many small incidents added over the years, brick-by-brick.

Her hand tightened on his arm, a gentle, warning pressure. Her eyes met his then flicked to a pair of gentlemen standing to one side. They were talking, not in low voices, but almost too loudly. A trifle foxed. Or nervous.

Blackerby nodded ever so slightly, and maneuvered them closer, stopping to chat with Spencer Perceval, the Prime Minister, who stood near enough to the men that Lady Amelia could eavesdrop on them.

After several minutes of Blackerby listening to the Prime Minister meticulously outline his concerns about a Luddite riot in the Midlands, Shade swung his head around with a low hiss, and Lady Amelia's fingers dug into Blackerby's arm.

"Do pardon me," he said, cutting Perceval off mid-sentence.

He turned to see where his dragon and Lady Amelia were looking. Prinny had stepped out of his circle of admirers to approach a woman much too young for the old lecher. The two men—one tall and angular and the other built like a pugilist—approached Prinny.

Blackerby dropped a questioning look to Lady Amelia.

"It sounded like them, but they didn't say anything incriminating," she whispered. "As soon as they saw their chance, though, they moved toward him."

He nodded and looked for Eliza Parry and Lord Westing. They were playing their parts exactly as he had instructed, staying near Prinny and watching for Blackerby's signal.

Blackerby dropped Lady Amelia's arm, hoping she had the sense to stay back. The shadows pooling around his feet stirred at his agitation then darted forward, happy to be unleashed, swirling around the two men like waves.

Onlookers gasped and pressed away from the shadows. The two men broke into a run. Directly for the Prince Regent.

Prinny froze, eyes wide. His dragon waddled between him and the approaching men and flared its wings. But if these were Luddite assassins, they could easily have other accomplices waiting to move in.

"Stop!" Blackerby called.

The men didn't stop, but that was the signal for his dragon-linked accomplices.

Shade launched from Blackerby's shoulder, flapping down to the pugilist and clamping onto his arm with his venomous bite. Eliza and Westing's dragons attacked the taller man, breathing steam and ice into his face.

The men smacked and flailed at the dragons, still struggling closer to Prinny.

Eliza gestured, and the liquid rose from her glass and the glasses of those around her. The mix of water, lemonade, and ratafia shot through the air to drench the floor around the men. Westing stepped forward, hand extended, and the liquid froze instantly, sending the men sprawling onto the slick floor.

The taller man clutched his elbow, but the pugilist scrambled forward and reached into his coat. Gasps and shouts rippled through the onlookers.

Blackerby leaped forward and wrenched the pugilist's arm behind him.

"Now there," Blackerby said quietly. "Perhaps you can talk to me about whatever it is that you feel is so urgent for the Prince Regent to hear."

They almost never fought him. Very few people would dare. But this man bared his teeth and tried to yank his arm away.

The taller man lurched forward over the ice, but Blackerby kicked out and caught him in the knee, and he fell flat on the floor. Lord Westing was quick to step in and put a foot on the tall man's back. The man rolled over and shoved Westing's foot, sending Westing slipping into Blackerby.

The pugilist broke free and reached once more into his coat. Blackerby rolled away from Westing and came up on his knees. He could not allow the man to pull out a weapon. In such a crowded room, it would almost certainly be fatal to someone. His eyes flicked to Lady Amelia, who watched with a pale face.

Blackerby wasn't a sportsman like Westing, but he'd spent enough time in the unsavory alleyways of London to know how to use an opponent's strength against him—and not to trust them to fight fair. He lunged for the pugilist, pinning him down and scrambling to find whatever he had hidden in his coat.

Westing, meanwhile, had wrestled the taller man into a headlock and seemed likely to squeeze him into unconsciousness.

Prinny still stood there like a dumb ox waiting to see if it would be slaughtered. His dragon blinked slowly and sat on its haunches.

Luckily, Blackerby had stationed a squad of his best Bow Street Runners outside, and they trickled into the edges of the crowd. Blackerby scanned the room, still expecting more assassins to melt out from among the onlookers.

The man Blackerby held managed to yank his hand free again. Blackerby grappled with the man, but Shade was ahead of him. The dragon leapt onto the man's back and sunk his teeth into his shoulder right beside his neck.

Blackerby grabbed the man by both arms and said, "It's interesting. Most dragons are not venomous, but mine is."

Still, the man did not relent. His eyes were beginning to glaze, and in a few moments, he would be sick as a dog. Blackerby patted down the man's coat and pulled out...

A folded piece of paper.

The pugilist turned his face to Prinny.

"A petition, Your Highness. It is time for the tyranny of the upper classes to stop," the pugilist rasped out. "Recognize our rights as citizens. We implore you to extend the right to vote to all the men of England whether we have dragons or not."

Prinny wrinkled his nose and stepped away from the man's petition. His dragon yawned, showing off a long, reptilian tongue.

The pugilist's eyes rolled back in his head, and he groaned as the full effects of the dragon venom coursed through his system. He wouldn't die, but he might wish he had for a few days.

Blackerby unfolded the paper, careful not to touch it with his bare skin. He would have it checked for poison, but he didn't think he would find any. It was, as the man had said, a petition. A quick search of the man and his accomplice, who had gone very still at the mention of venom, revealed they had nothing worse about their persons than cheap snuff.

Blackerby wanted to kick both men for good measure, but everyone was watching, and he would look foolish. More foolish.

Prinny dabbed his forehead with a handkerchief. "Good work, Blackerby! I don't know how these ruffians sneaked in, but we don't need any of their Whig politics here."

Blackerby inclined his head. This was not what he was supposed to be doing. Let them annoy Prinny. It was better that than turn against him completely, which is what they would do if he didn't learn to make some concessions.

His runners finally broke through the gossiping crowd, and Blackerby handed the men over to them as if this is what he had planned all along. Then he went off to stew over his embarrassment. All that effort wasted on a couple of Whigs with a petition when he knew the Luddites were planning something. Something big.

Lady Amelia caught up with his long strides, practically jogging to do so. He sighed and slowed his pace.

"I'm sorry," she said.

He glanced down at her. Her eyes shone with worry.

"It's not your fault," he said. "You told me what you heard, and the men very well *could* have been planning an attack based on what we knew."

"Do you think they were connected to the Luddites?"

He stopped and frowned. He and Lady Amelia were in a quiet corridor, out of earshot of most of the party. "It's possible. I'm skeptical, though."

"Do people try to approach Pri—the Prince Regent often? Asking for help?"

"Honestly, anyone who knows Prinny knows he won't be much help to them unless, perhaps, it involves patronage of the arts. And even then, he'll mostly be of use to himself."

"But your spies told you there would be an attempt on the Prince Regent's life."

"Hmm. Actually, no. I only knew that they were planning something big this week. I thought you had provided the clue."

"Then they could be planning something else."

In the frustration of the moment, he hadn't stopped to think about it, but now a cold feeling slithered through his stomach. "I'm afraid they might be. Perhaps something tonight, while everyone is at this blasted party."

Were these two men an intentional distraction? Blackerby turned to leave, to touch base with his Runners. He had drawn too many of them from other assignments to bring them to the party.

A thundering boom shook the corridor and rattled the crystal chandelier above them, sending broken rainbows of reflected light skittering over the walls. Instinctively, Blackerby drew Lady Amelia close. And she leaned into him, as though she trusted him. Indeed, she had never seemed afraid of him as so many were.

"What was that?" she asked.

Blackerby swore under his breath and loosened his grip on her. "I don't know, but I believe the Luddites have struck their blow."

Chapter Seven

BLACKERBY STRODE OUTSIDE, vaguely aware that Lady Amelia was running to keep up with him. Many of the rest of the party followed, though Lord Westing had the sense to keep Prinny back. The crowds parted to let Blackerby through, many looking to him to see how he would react. In the distance, fire sirens went off, and an orange glow blazed to the southeast.

Brainy Jamie ran up with David the street sweep. They'd been keeping watch on the streets as Blackerby had requested.

"Fire, my lord!" Brainy Jamie panted. "At Westminster."

Westminster. The seat of Parliament.

Blackerby swore eloquently, disregarding Lady Amelia's presence. She didn't flinch. His dragon hopped about in agitation, and shadows rotated around him like a gathering tornado.

"What happened?" Lady Amelia asked.

"The Luddites have taken a page from their forebearers' book. I would bet on gunpowder. We are probably fortunate that they chose to attack at night when no one would be in Parliament."

"How considerate of them," Amelia said drily.

"Wasn't it, though?" He furrowed his brow. "But the Luddites are not considerate." He would need to question the two petitioners, see if they were part of the scheme—a distraction—even unwittingly. And he needed to see what was left of Westminster. He looked back to Lady Amelia. "I dislike leaving you when I may have drawn you into danger, but I'm needed elsewhere."

"Of course. I'm sure my mother is in hysterics, but the Westings will help us home."

Yes, they would. Westing was such a perfect little stone knight, after all. Of course, he had been handy in the fight with the petitioners.

Blackerby bowed and turned his back on Lady Amelia and the party to run for Westminster. The streets would be too crowded with fire wagons and spectators for him to be able to ride there.

As Blackerby raced through the night, shadows whispered to him of danger, danger, danger. He wanted to shout back that he didn't need their hints. London's flickering red skyline and the thick stench of smoke were enough.

By the time he arrived at Westminster, the fire had burst through the windows, and the roof of the ancient palace blazed yellow and orange. The House of Lords' chamber was fully engulfed. Even over the shouts of the fire brigades, the roar of the flames and the cracking of wood beams and hot stones sounded in the night like the keening of the dying building.

Blackerby shielded his eyes against the blaze. Black smoke blotted out the moon and stars, so the only light came from the great fire, as though they were trapped in a prison of flames and soot. Glowing embers drifted down from the sky down to sizzle on his evening jacket. He slapped them out. Crankshaw, his valet, would be heartbroken over the ruined jacket.

Crowds gathered to stare in stunned quiet, some even spectating from boats along the Thames. The flames' reflection glowed over the black of the water. Fire wagons pumped water to put the fire out—aided, he saw, by Eliza Parry and her dragon beside the river—and bucket brigades lined up along the Thames, passing pails of water, though they looked like ants trying to defeat a lion.

Many of the passersby did not seem very sorry to see Parliament burn. Several artists even set up canvases to draw or paint the scene.

Cold washed over Blackerby despite the heat crackling from the flames.

The onlookers were rapt at the site of the burning building, but Blackerby needed to get closer. He had only to extend the shadows around him, which were happy to slither through the crowd, and a way parted to let him through. People turned their faces away, perhaps afraid that he had sensed their glee at watching the government burn. He wanted to shout at them that chaos would benefit no one, but they would not listen. Instead, he pressed his way forward to the line of soldiers holding the crowd back. Even they did not stand in his way.

He stood and watched for a moment as the fire brigades worked to save the rest of Westminster, but then he had to avert his face from the heat stinging his cheeks.

"The roof is going!" one of the fire brigades shouted nearby.

The people fighting the fire pressed back. Blackerby squinted up in time to see the burning timber roof give in and crash down into the hungry flames. The fire seemed to roar in triumph, and smoke and debris exploded from the gaping windows and doorways. A ball of fire blasted into the night.

Some in the audience whistled or snickered. He thought he heard cheers from the river. Both houses of government would be lost.

Feeling ill, Blackerby turned away. Westminster was a hopeless cause, but he had to try to save what he could. He spotted one of his Runners among the constables trying to hold back to crowds. He gestured the man over.

"We need other dragon-linked attuned to water and wind to help with the fire. Send someone for Lord Henry, James Borne, and Lady Ashley. Oh, and Mrs. Reynolds in Bond Street. She is attuned to fire. Perhaps she can help control it."

The Runner nodded and dashed off to relay the order. Blackerby paced.

It was far too convenient that the Luddites had not attacked while the houses of government met. Did they just want to send a message? Was this the only time they could plan their blast?

Blackerby turned his back on the conflagration that had overtaken what was once a scene of power and triumph for him, though the heat still crept through his jacket and made his shoulders itch. The fire's orange flames reflected off the stained glass of Westminster Abbey.

William Vincent, the dean of the Abbey, ran up to him, his jowly face smudged with ash or dirt, and his old-fashioned white wig hanging askance.

"Luddites!" the dean cried. "They tried to blow up the Abbey, too."

Blackerby's eyes narrowed. It was one thing to destroy a representation of government. But a church? And a burial place at that? The dead ought to be left in peace. The shadows swirled around him, a whirlpool of agitation.

"Show me," he ordered.

The dean ran ahead, leading Blackerby across the street to Westminster Abbey. The glass was smashed out of the windows in the cloister, and a hole gaped in the wall where the door had been. "Here, you see!"

Blackerby stepped through the jagged gap and let his eyes adjust to the dim light coming from the burning Parliament buildings. Chunks of stone and glass shards littered the ancient building, but otherwise, the damage appeared minimal.

"There was no fire here?" Blackerby asked the dean, who stood wringing his hands.

"No, but see how they've defiled it."

Someone had painted a crude image of a lance on the abbey floor. The sign of the Luddites and their hero, St. George the dragon slayer. A year ago, Blackerby had thought that was just a legend, but now he knew that dragons could be killed. The Luddites knew it, too. All they needed was the elemental object linked to the dragon.

If the Luddites had time to paint a lance on the floor, they had time to burn the abbey, but they didn't. They wanted something else here.

Blackerby thought of the great White Dragon asleep beneath the Tower of London, and the shadows of the Abbey seemed to close in on him, gripping his stomach with iron bands of dread. If the White Dragon died, England would fall, or so the legends said. What was its elemental object? Was it in the Abbey?

He drew a deep breath and forced the darkness from his mind. The White Dragon of England was much older than the abbey and the kings and queens turning to dust in their sepulchers, ancient as they were. No, the White Dragon's object would be some Celtic or Roman treasure. A sword or piece of jewelry perhaps. Maybe something in the British Museum, if the object wasn't still buried with the dragon. Blackerby would have to increase the guard at the museum and the Tower of London. The damage to the abbey might be another distraction.

"Did they desecrate the graves?" Blackerby asked.

"No, but they tore out sacred ornaments and defaced the church."

"Did they steal anything? The ornaments they tore down?"

The dean's face went pale under the dirt smudging it. "I think it likely, my lord. I haven't made a full inventory. In all the chaos… As soon as I raised the alarm about the intruders, Parliament went up in flames."

Blackerby watched the odd, distorted images of the flames dancing through the ancient windows. "They attacked the Abbey first, then created a distraction."

"My lord?"

"I want to know as soon as possible what has been stolen."

He didn't share his thoughts with Dean Vincent. For all he knew, the man had been involved. There were spies all about them, and he still didn't know how the Luddites were getting their inside information. Had they had help planning this attack, or whatever it was? As much as he wanted to talk it over with someone, he could not. An image of Lady Amelia flashed in his mind, but he shook his head. No distractions. He had to retreat up the street to his Whitehall offices, touch base with any Runners who were about the city. Get this sorted. The Luddites were still a step ahead of him.

Chapter Eight

AMELIA COULDN'T SLEEP. Not while the city burned so near that the flames and smoke smudged an endless Armageddon dusk across the sky and stung her eyes. Not while she wondered if she could have done more to prevent it. If Shaw had used her somehow.

She should have stuck with writing her gossip tales. Mockery was her only skill. She was not one of the shining dragon-linked with powers that let them bend the elements. She was not even master of her own life or future.

The papers on her desk took on a dull orange hue in the nightmarish light filtering through the window. Perhaps writing would distract her. But when she sat and picked up her pen, rehashing the daily gossip into silly stories did not appeal to her much. Instead, she turned and watched out her window, wondering what Blackerby had discovered.

She dozed off in her chair to be awakened by a timid knock on her door.

She jolted awake with a guilty start. What had happened while she slept?

"Enter," she called, rubbing the sleep from her eyes.

The butler pushed the door open, looking apologetic.

Amelia stood. She still wore the gown from the night before, though it was now terribly rumpled. "Moore, it must be early. I assume there is news."

"It all seems... the same out there, my lady. But Lady Millicent is here. I told her you were likely sleeping, but she is overwrought."

Amelia sighed. "See her in."

Millicent tore into the room, her dragon flapping about in agitation. It landed on the windowsill, panting. Millicent took Amelia's hands, gripping them tightly.

"My friend, speak words of comfort to me." Millicent's expression looked sincere without any hint of posturing. "Everyone is in a panic. Pierre... Mr. Moreau... says it is just like France. But I've heard you were there last night. With Lord Blackerby. When everything started."

Thus, the spears of gossip turned on Amelia. She helped Millicent on her settee and patted her hand. "I was at the party when we all heard the explosion. All I know is that the Luddites attacked Westminster."

Millicent reached out a hand for her dragon, and the creature flapped over to nestle in her lap. "It feels as though the world is ending. My parents are in an utter panic. Randolph went out last night before it happened, probably to some gambling hell, and he hasn't returned. Two of our servants left this morning—said they wouldn't be around the dragon-linked and just walked away. I was only able to convince my maid to come here with me by reminding her that your family has no dragon-linked members. I left the useless thing to nap in your drawing room." Her face softened. "But Pierre says he will keep me safe, since he has survived revolution before."

Amelia rubbed her friend's back. "Pierre" was certainly full of wisdom. "Where is Mr. Moreau now?"

She hesitated, like she was holding something back. Then she said, "He went to see if the fire is out. He is so brave."

"Hmm." Mr. Moreau had often been near when the Luddites struck. They attacked his party last Season, and he was at Lyme Regis when Shaw tried to kill or control the water dragon there. But Amelia had been at both places as well. It didn't necessarily mean anything. And Millicent would never help the Luddites.

"I will find us some tea," Amelia said.

She went into the corridor to summon a maid or footman. She found Jane pacing there, her face lined with tears.

"Jane," Amelia said. "Something has upset you."

Jane stared at her as if she were a ghost. "Lady Amelia!" She broke into shuddering sobs.

Amelia was tempted to put Millicent and Jane in the room together and let them outcry each other, but kindness won out, and she drew Jane into an empty guest room. "Tell me what happened."

"There was a m-man," Jane said between sniffles. "He... Oh, my lady, it is too terrible to say!"

Amelia's fingers went cold, and she curled them into her skirt. "He hurt you."

"No! He asked me to hurt *you*. To put poison in your drink. He said if I did not, or if I told you, he would kill me. But I can't do it. I won't." She put her face in her hands and sobbed.

Amelia stared at the maid. She felt as though ice were creeping over her body, turning her arms and legs numb and forming a hard lump in her stomach. Mechanically, she patted Jane on the back. Was this Amelia's earlier attacker resorting to new methods? Or had someone else taken it into their heads to murder her?

"No one will kill you," Amelia said. She would make sure of that. "You did right to tell me. What did the man look like?"

Jane trembled all over. "He wore a terrible white mask, and his voice was low and grating, like it came from the devil himself."

Amelia shivered and glanced over her shoulder, as though the terrible mask might be hovering behind her, eyes watching from the expressionless white face. Though, at least it sounded like she only had one mortal enemy. "He gave you the poison, I imagine. What did you do with it?"

"I left it in the pantry with the rat poison. I didn't want anyone unsuspecting to touch it."

"An excellent plan. You've had a trying time. Lie down and rest on the bed in here."

"Thank you, my lady," Jane said through her tears.

Amelia returned to the corridor and leaned against the wall. A portrait of some female ancestor regarded her with a painted-on smile.

"You never had these problems," Amelia accused her.

She shut her eyes to think. This was beyond anything she could handle. She needed Lord Blackerby. Warmth blossomed in her chest as she thought of him coming to her rescue, but she quickly squelched any such notions. First, Blackerby was not the heroic knight sort. Second, he was rather occupied now with Westminster burning. Amelia's problem would seem small in comparison. But Amelia was not self-sacrificing enough to ignore a third attempt on her life, especially when the villain was now stalking her house, threatening her servants.

Amelia sneaked downstairs and opened the front door. The strange hazy orange still hung over the city, and she could not be certain of the time, but the little street sweep wandered the green with his broom. In fact, he was the only one about in Grosvenor Square.

Amelia checked to be sure no one was lurking in the shadows and motioned for the boy. After a moment, he caught her gesture and hurried over.

"You, lad," she said. "What is your name?"

"David, miss."

"David, I would like you to take a message to Lord Blackerby. Can you do that for me?"

He hesitated until she produced a shilling, then he nodded eagerly.

"Tell him…" She did not want to disclose too much, even to a boy she felt certain was in Blackerby's employ. "Tell him Lady Amelia needs to speak with him urgently."

"Yes, miss!" And David was off.

Amelia sighed heavily. She could not know how long it would be before Blackerby would speak to her. In the meantime, she would have a frank discussion with Cook about watching the food. Their cook had no desire to see the family poisoned, but Amelia could not be sure who else she could trust.

Blackerby, she thought. As strange as it seemed, she trusted Blackerby.

Chapter Nine

BLACKERBY STAYED OUT IN WHITEHALL, coordinating with his Runners until the fire brigades and the dragon-linked had contained the fire. Westminster Palace still smoked—it would for days as the fire burned itself out—but the fire didn't spread past the palace, and old Westminster Hall might be salvaged. A layer of ash smothered everything, turning the world gray.

With the initial danger from the fire gone, Blackerby's energy disappeared as well. He was not interested in trekking through the ash, or in putting on a clean suit that would be ruined by the soot. He shut the curtains, for once welcoming the quiet of the dark, and stretched out on the sofa to catch what rest was appointed to the wicked.

When someone tapped on his door a while later, he was instantly awake.

"Enter," he called, not bothering to make himself more presentable. No one would be at their best that morning.

Farris shuffled in, his face smudged with soot and his curly red hair in chaos. He showed no surprise at seeing his master in similar dirt. "My lord."

"Well?" Blackerby asked, rising to his feet.

"We know what was taken from Westminster Abbey."

"Already? I expected it would take ages to inventory everything in that ancient pile."

"As they cleaned up, they saw that only one thing was missing."

Blackerby did not like the sound of that. "What might that be?"

"The Stone of Scone."

"The... the Stone of Scone?"

"The Stone of Destiny, some call it. It was the stone used by Scottish kings for their coronations. King Edward removed it from Scotland in—"

"Yes, I know what it is. It must weigh hundreds of pounds."

"Over three hundred, my lord."

"One person would be hard pressed to steal it themselves. Magic wouldn't do it."

"Yes, my lord. It must have taken at least two strong men. Perhaps more, bearing it on a litter."

"Hmm."

Blackerby rubbed his eyes, realizing too late he had probably just streaked soot across his face. This whole debacle had been about the Stone of Destiny, then. Why did the Luddites want it so badly? It couldn't be the White Dragon's object—it wasn't old enough and was from the wrong country.

Maybe Shaw wished to be crowned king of Scotland, establish his own breakaway kingdom? There were fewer dragons there. The Scots, and later the Jacobites, had never cared much for dragons, preferring bloodlines over magic. But the Jacobites' power had waned significantly in the last generation. Still, that could be Shaw's angle: better to reign in hell than to serve in heaven or some rot like that. Not that Scotland was *that* bad, but the weather... Blackerby shivered.

He would have to retrieve the stone, of course. The Luddites moved it under the cover of the fire. Carried it... No. They would have shuffled off to the Thames with it and sailed away. It was long gone now. Still, he had contacts in Scotland.

Blackerby glanced up at his faithful Runner. "You are of Scots extraction, are you not, Farris?"

"I was born in Kirkcudbright, my lord. Moved to Glasgow and then London as a lad."

"What do you know of the Stone of Scone?"

"Just the same as any Scottish schoolboy might. It was blessed by St. Patrick and was the coronation seat of the first king of the Scots. Kenneth MacAlpine and all the Scottish kings after him sat on it to be coronated until bloody Edward Longshanks stole it and brought it to England."

"And now that the kingdoms are united, it once again hosts royal bottoms when their heads are crowned," Blackerby mused. "I'm certain Prinny wishes to use it as well when the king succumbs to his afflictions."

Farris huffed at that, but Blackerby chose not to pursue any treasonous thoughts entertained by his subordinate. He had plenty of his own.

Farris looked thoughtful as he stared at the curtained window, then he said, "It may not be the real one, you know. Many folks think the monks switched it before Edward hauled it off. Say it might be an old privy cover." He snickered at that, and Blackerby smiled as well. "Besides, the real one is supposed to whisper the name of the rightful king when someone of royal blood sits on it, and they say that such a king would have control even over the chaos of the elements."

"That would be a fine thing," Blackerby said. "Certainly, a skill our monarchs seem to lack." His smile faltered as Farris's words set in. "Is chaos an element?"

"Seems that way sometimes."

"No, stop. Think about this. Darkness and light are elements linked to dragon magic. I have heard rumors of a lad attuned to luck. Could chaos be a magical element as well?"

Farris reflected on that. "I'm not dragon-linked and don't know that much about it, but I don't see why it couldn't be."

"What Scottish great dragons do you know of? What are they attuned to?"

"There's a water dragon and a lightning dragon, least according to the stories."

"Were they tied to any of your kings in the past? Were those early kings dragon-linked?"

"I don't think so. That was never as important to the Scots. We saw the dragons as a nuisance mostly. Some of the kings probably were dragon-linked, but we don't have as many legends about that as the English do."

Blackerby drew a deep breath. "I will need to talk to my dragon expert. If there is a chaos dragon, Shaw may now have the object that would let him control it. Or kill it. What would that do?"

A dull headache pushed behind Blackerby's eyes. The cloying stench of smoke and the haze of exhaustion clouded his mind. Eliza Parry had been able to communicate with the great water dragon near Lyme Regis, but she was also attuned to water. The Westing ancestors who had tried to control the earth dragon had killed it.

Maybe that was all Shaw wanted. If there was a dragon attuned to chaos, he might wish to kill it. Blackerby wasn't fond of chaos unless he could use it in his favor, but he didn't think the destruction of any element would be healthy for the nation. Did Shaw just want to hurt England in any way possible? Perhaps the stone was the only dragon's object he could find.

That was assuming the Stone of Scone was a dragon's object. This could still be a bid to create a Scottish rebellion. The headache pulsed, a sharp pain behind one eye. Blackerby needed more information, and the shadows were not helpful. He would dredge his network of spies for any clues.

A scuffling from the corridor broke his train of thought, and a sharp knock sounded.

"Enter," Blackerby called.

One of his Runners maneuvered into the room hauling a scruffy little boy by the collar. Blackerby's scalp prickled when he recognized the lad as the street sweep, David.

"I caught this urchin lurking about," the Runner panted.

"You may let him go," Blackerby said. "He reports to me."

He turned his gaze on the boy, whose face was flushed from struggling against the Runner. David shot a triumphant look at the man.

"I said 'is lordship would be wishful to see me, didn't I?"

"But why have you left your post?" Blackerby asked, a coldness settling in his stomach. The boy's only job was to watch the Hayes' house.

"That flash mort you 'ad me watching—"

"The 'flash mort' is a lady."

"Sorry, 'course she is. Well, the lady marched right out of the 'ouse and told me to get a message to you. Said she 'ad something urgent to tell."

"Do you know about what?"

"She didn't say. But there'd been some commotion in the 'ouse. Another lady showed up with a maid, all bawling and carrying on."

"Hmm. You've done well." Blackerby flicked a coin to the boy. "Now, back to your post. I will be along soon." The boy hurried out with a wide grin, and Blackerby turned back to Farris. "Get every Runner on the force. Send them to ground to search for any hint about the stone or trouble in Scotland. We must get ahead of Shaw."

"Yes, my lord." Farris didn't ask, but Blackerby saw the question in his eyes.

"I will be conducting my own investigations. Lady Amelia is 'flash' indeed, and she's not given to exaggeration. I'm going to see what information she has for us. We need anything we can find that will lead us to Shaw."

Chapter Ten

AMELIA FINALLY SAW Lady Millicent off with her maid and the gallant Pierre Moreau. Amelia spared him a speculative glance, but then she needed to check on Jane. Her maid was sleeping soundly. Fortunate girl.

A jumpy-looking Moore found Amelia in the corridor.

"I'm sorry to disturb you, my lady, but your father has locked himself in the study, and your mother is... indisposed."

"I would imagine," Amelia said. She wondered what it was like to have the luxury to be indisposed whenever things were inconvenient. "Tell me the problem."

"One of the footmen seems to have left without permission."

One less person in the household who might try to poison Amelia. She took a deep breath. "He may have panicked. If he's not back in a day or two, we'll see about replacing him."

She hoped things were normal enough in a few days that replacing servants was their only concern.

"In the meantime," she said, "tell me immediately if you hear of any other... discontent or concerns among the household." As in, planning to murder Lady Amelia. But she was afraid mentioning that to Moore would only panic him further.

"Yes, my lady." Moore nodded and wandered off.

Amelia retreated to her room and shut her door, leaning against it as if she could keep out the burning city and the people who wanted her dead. The door was solid oak, but it did not seem quite as sturdy as it once had.

A timid knock sounded on her door.

"Yes?" Amelia called, dreading whatever news came next.

Moore poked his head in, looking pale and disconcerted. "My lady, Lord Blackerby is here. He wishes to speak to you. I told him it was highly irregular."

Amelia almost laughed in relief. "I would say this is an irregular day."

She swept past the stammering butler and found Lord Blackerby in the drawing-room, his shadows making themselves at home in the corners. His face looked freshly cleaned, but his clothes—his evening jacket from the night before—carried the heavy scent of smoke. He came forward and bowed, his eyes tired but curious and intense.

"You summoned me, my lady, and you see, I have arrived."

Something in her chest fluttered at his words. He had come to see her even before changing his clothes. He had come to her rescue. "Thank you. I hate to trouble you, my lord, but I was not sure..." She suddenly felt very silly for not being able to deal with the problem herself. What if he thought she had news of Shaw and was disappointed in her for bothering him? Why could she not take control of her own destiny for once?

"Tell me," he urged, his deep voice serious for once.

"My maid tells me that a man in a bauta mask both bribed and threatened her to poison me. She reported it to me, but I am concerned."

His eyes grew hard, and he took out his quizzing glass, turning it in his fingers. "Yes. It is concerning. Three attempts on your life—one before the conversation you overheard at the party, and one the same night that Parliament burned. Someone is very anxious to be rid of you. It must be something that you know."

She raised her hands helplessly. "But I can think of nothing I know that would be damaging to anyone. Even whatever I thought I heard at the costume ball seems to have been a false lead."

Blackerby shook his head. "Those two men escaped. A group of ruffians overwhelmed the Runners who had them in custody. They likely are linked to a larger plot, but it has to be more than a distraction over the fire last night, since they attacked you again after." He looked thoughtful for a moment, then turned to her. "Even that was a diversion. The real reason for the fire seems to have been the opportunity to steal the Stone of Scone."

Amelia wrinkled her forehead. "The one kings sit on when they are crowned."

"Yes. And, perhaps, an object with a link to a dragon, though I do not yet know for certain. My concern is that the Luddites seem to have an inside source—someone from the upper ranks who is helping them. I do not yet know who, but I wonder if you have stumbled upon the villain without realizing it."

"But that's ridiculous. How can I reveal them if I don't even know who the person is? And I don't think I know any secrets that others don't."

A thump drew their attention to Shade, who had hopped onto the desk and knocked over several of Miss Charity's volumes.

Blackerby grinned. "But unlike others, you broadcast those secrets to the world. Which book was published just before the first attack?"

Amelia shook her head, thinking that Blackerby was on the wrong track, but since she had no other ideas, she handed him the correct volume.

He flipped through the pages. "I think the key is in here. The person who is trying to kill you."

"I thought we had settled that no one would murder me over being embarrassed in a book."

"Not being embarrassed. Being exposed. You have a knack for character, my lady, and I think you sometimes capture more than you realize."

"I don't recall a spy in any of my stories."

"No, and I think that's why he has not been in more of a hurry to kill you. Either he was not entirely sure you were the author, or he was not entirely sure you had realized who he was. But enough information was there for him to recognize it, and for him to fear that others would, too."

"But who? I am still mystified."

"As I am, because I remember this volume, and I can pick out who is acting as a traitor, but not who he represents in reality."

"Well?"

"The Swan Knight."

Amelia stared at him, her eyes wide. "You cannot be serious. He's a boorish idiot!"

"He seems to be, but you have shown him playing the traitor as well. He recognized himself, though I cannot decipher him. Come, who is it?"

Amelia sat, her tongue feeling heavy and her head spinning in confusion. This could not be. She felt like the traitor now. But dark ash fluttered past the windows like filthy snow, a reminder of what was at stake. She could not deny Blackerby the help he needed. And she realized it made sense. The pieces fit together. Someone who moved in the right circles. Who had been present at all the right times. Who chafed at authority.

Amelia met his eyes. "Randolph. The Swan Knight—the traitor—is Randolph Blanchfield."

Blackerby stood, his eyes bright with excitement. "You have been most helpful, my lady. Thank you. This should put you beyond the reach of danger soon."

"Because you will apprehend him." All she could think was that she had not been as clever as she imagined. She had teased Randolph about looking like a swan when they were younger, with that long neck of his. He had not forgotten, and now he knew that she was Miss Charity. And this was how he reacted?

"Naturally, I will catch him," Blackerby said. "As soon as possible. We cannot have him causing any more uproars."

"I want to help."

"I hardly think that is wise, seeing as the man has tried to kill you. Thrice."

Amelia shuddered at that. "I never saw him. Maybe Shaw sent someone to do it. Randolph wouldn't actually harm me."

"Lady Amelia—"

"He was my friend! Not like his sister, but I have known them both all my life."

A strange look passed over Blackerby's eyes.

Amelia covered her mouth. "No, do not say that Millicent is involved in this as well!" But Millicent had fallen under the sway of Pierre Moreau, and Amelia had wondered if he might be involved with the Luddites.

"I don't know," Blackerby said with surprising gentleness. "I will have to determine how far the Blanchfields' deception reaches."

"But Millicent is dragon-linked!"

"That has not always stopped people from being resentful."

The room swayed underfoot, and Amelia covered her mouth. "I think I'm going to be sick."

"Then you definitely should stay here."

Amelia turned on him, trying to decipher his expression. "How can you be so callous! My own friends—spies—and outed by myself!"

"Do you regret revealing them?" Blackerby's lips quirked, no doubt hiding whatever his real thoughts were on the matter.

"I don't know," Amelia admitted. "You can't imagine what it has been like, growing up as confined as we did. Not allowed to even have our own thoughts. I escaped through writing. How can I blame them if they found some other way to lash out at people who denied them every chance to be happy?"

Blackerby looked thoughtful. "If they were merely choosing to make unsuitable matches or ruin their family name, I would have no judgment to pass on them, but they are involved with Shaw, and you have some inkling of what he is."

Amelia groaned and sank back into the sofa. "A terrible mistake. It must have been a terrible mistake. Maybe he lured them in and now they cannot escape his clutches."

"That is possible," Blackerby relented. "I cannot allow Randolph Blanchfield—or his sister—to cause any more havoc, but I can try to see to what extent they might have been drawn in unawares. There will have to be consequences for their actions, though."

Amelia squeezed her eyes shut and nodded. Randolph wasn't dragon-linked, but Millicent was. The penalty for dragon-linked traitors was gruesome and unforgiving, more so than run-of-the-mill traitors against the crown.

"You know you cannot see them for the time being."

"Of course, I know that!" What an impossible, arrogant man. Thinking that she was a fool.

She had been a fool, though. Not as clever as she thought. And a part of her regretted that she had given herself away and gotten her friends into trouble, even if they were involved in something terrible. She could only console herself with the hope that they had been tricked. Especially if Millicent were entangled as well, with the threat of being labeled a dragon-linked traitor hanging over her head. Like a guillotine blade.

"I saw Millicent just this morning," Amelia said dully. "She did not act guilty, but she did mention she has been spending time with Pierre Moreau."

"Ah, yes, I have had my eye on him for some time."

"She also mentioned that her family has not seen her brother since before the fire. He never returned home after that."

Blackerby's eyes glittered. "That does sound promising." His expression softened as he looked at her. "I know this must be difficult, my dear. You are doing the right thing by helping your country, and if Lady Millicent has been tricked into being involved, I will do everything I can to soften the consequences for her."

Amelia released a shuddering breath and reached out a hand. "Thank you, my lord. I know it is very wrong of her, and she has become a difficult person, but she was not always thus."

He took her hand and squeezed it, his grip warm and strong and surprisingly comforting. "It is not easy when one has been dealt a poor hand, though we do have to play the cards we hold as well as we can."

"Of course, I realize that." Though Amelia wondered if she had played her hand well. She was trapped by her parents' expectations, their strict constraints, but inventing Miss Charity was beginning to seem like a foolish reaction.

Yet Blackerby did not look at her—or treat her—like the fool she felt. Instead, his face was full of sympathy. It made Amelia feel both terribly vulnerable and wonderfully safe, a novel sensation that she wanted to get lost in.

The door to the drawing room burst open, and Lord Hayes stormed in, face red with fury.

Amelia's breath caught, and she tightened her grip on Lord Blackerby's hand, even knowing that she should have separated herself from him instead. Still, she was grateful that he did not let go.

"Scoundrel! Menace!" Her father bore down on Lord Blackerby until Shade slithered forward, teeth bared. Lord Hayes stopped, but he pointed at the earl. "Seducer! How dare you come here and abuse my daughter in this manner?" He turned on Amelia. "How dare you put yourself in such a compromising position when it is already so difficult to find anyone willing to take you?"

Amelia shut her eyes and let her hand go limp in Blackerby's. Now, her humiliation was complete. Perhaps she should find Randolph and ask him to finish his task quickly.

But Blackerby tightened his grip and pulled her to her feet, drawing her close. Near enough that she could smell his sandalwood scent beneath lingering hints of smoke from the night's fire. She looked at him in confusion, but his smirk was fixed on her father.

"I thought you would want to congratulate us, my lord," Blackerby said, his voice mocking.

"You…" Lord Hayes' face went from angry to confused to cunning. "You're going to take her off my hands?"

"Indeed," Blackerby said. "Immediately."

Amelia did her best not to gape at him. What was he saying? He did not actually want to marry her. She enjoyed seeing her father discomfited, but when the jest was over, what became of her then?

"I've never cared for you, Lord Blackerby," Lord Hayes said. "But perhaps Amelia will teach you your duty."

"Oh, I'm certain she will," Blackerby purred, wrapping his arm around Amelia's shoulders. "For now, I will be removing her to stay with the Westings. I'm sure you would rather not have to see me in your home again."

"Do what you like with her," Lord Hayes said, his eyes glittering. "I'll send my solicitor to yours to draw up the settlement contract." He stomped out of the room without another look at his daughter.

Amelia pulled away from Blackerby, heat prickling over her skin. She couldn't even say if she was more embarrassed or angry, or if there was something else about the way he held her that had made her flush so. "What on earth—"

"You can scold me later, my dear." Blackerby smiled. "For now, fetch your loyal maid—perhaps the only person in this house who is not going to poison you—" he cast a nasty glance after her father "—and whatever things you require for a stay with the Westings."

"You're really taking me there?"

"You clearly cannot stay here, and I think you'll find their house well-guarded." He smiled in a way that warned her there was more to his plan than he was saying.

"I don't wish to be any trouble to them."

His eyes twinkled at some private jest. "My dear, I think you will find that you are the least of the Westings' troubles."

Chapter Eleven

BLACKERBY HAD ALWAYS KNOWN the darkness would someday drive him mad, and it had finally happened. Why else would he have dragged Lady Amelia into a false engagement?

Not that he minded the idea. In fact, it surprised him how easily it had come. He enjoyed flirting, but it was only a game to him, and everyone knew it. He didn't let emotion play a part in his actions, influenced as he was by darkness. But when he had seen Amelia's abuse by her father, the instinct to protect her had overwhelmed his common sense.

He checked his pocket watch, anxious for Amelia to collect her things so he could take her to safety. He couldn't imagine that she fancied this charade. No one worth having wanted to ally themselves with darkness. She would no doubt cry off later and leave him jilted. A shock of pain jolted him, but he shook it off. It was all he could expect —all he deserved. He didn't care what the gossips would say about him, and the midst of a national crisis was hardly the time to even think of such things.

There never would be a time that Blackerby could think of them. Duty always had to come first. But he had put Lady Amelia in what appeared to be a compromising position. Blackerby sometimes forgot the rules that governed the lives of ladies, especially when they became his co-conspirators. And none of them had ever been like Lady Amelia.

At least he had already planned to bring her to the Westings—the safest place he could think of in London, short of his own residence or St. James Palace. With her safe, he could focus on finding Randolph Blanchfield. He'd never trusted the man. Now, he knew why. And if Lady Millicent and Pierre Moreau were involved as well, he could stop them and cripple Shaw's information network.

He should have been triumphant. He was certain he had unmasked the traitor. And the traitor might lead him to Shaw. But Lady Amelia's distress gnawed at him. He normally didn't care what others thought of his work, but to see stoic Lady Amelia upset was disconcerting.

Never mind. He only had to track Randolph, determine if his banshee of a sister was involved as well, and he could put a stop to Shaw's plans.

It did not matter who the criminal was or who they were friends with.

Then why did he feel uneasy?

He put his pocket watch away and smiled when Amelia and her wide-eyed maid descended the stairs with several trunks and band boxes. Lady Amelia traveled relatively lightly. She probably guessed she would not be trekking into Society while at the Westings. No, the idea would be to lie low.

Amelia looked at him, her eyes full of questions, but this was not the time to discuss his plans, and some of them were too ill-formed to be put into words. Jane gaped at him and side-stepped his shadow companions. Amelia walked right across them, apparently having grown accustomed to them. Blackerby felt an unaccountable sense of pleasure at her lack of concern. Sensible girl.

They took his carriage to the Westings, accompanied by Farris and David the street sweep. The boy could do more good working with Brainy Jamie now that Lady Amelia was not at home. And they were obvious enough about relocating Lady Amelia that any of Shaw's spies would know she had moved and leave Grosvenor Square in peace.

Blackerby half-expected an attack on the way, but they made the short trip to Berkeley Square without incident.

Phoebe Westing looked only a little surprised when her butler announced the party.

"Lady Westing," Blackerby said, keeping a protective grip on Lady Amelia's elbow. "I have brought another guest to share the sanctuary of your home."

A moment of distress flashed in her eyes, no doubt wondering where she would put the new guests, but she was too kind-hearted, and her lord too practical, to turn away a friend in distress.

Joshua, Lord Westing's young half-brother, trotted down the stairs but stopped to gawk at the shadows creeping across the entryway. He placed his good hand on the banister—the other having been lost in a magical accident years before—and crept closer, obviously hoping Phoebe wouldn't notice him and send him away from whatever excitement was brewing.

"Of course, come in, Lady Amelia," Phoebe said. "Your maid may have to share your room, but perhaps that is safer if you're in some danger?"

Lady Amelia gave Blackerby a half-pleading look at Phoebe's unasked question. He raised his eyebrows at her. She should know that he would not spill her secrets, and Phoebe would not pry about the details of how Lady Amelia had come to be in danger.

"Thank you, Lady Westing," he said. "Lady Amelia has come across some information that may help us stop Shaw, but I'm afraid it also puts her in danger from the Luddites."

"No!" Phoebe gasped. She took Lady Amelia's arm and pulled her farther into the house, as if Luddites might be lurking on the street.

"She can stop my uncle?" Deborah Shaw came bounding out of the drawing-room and threw her arms around Lady Amelia, who froze in response. Deborah, seemingly oblivious to her discomfort, kissed her cheeks. "I am so happy. I would do anything to see him stopped." She turned to Phoebe with the expression of a martyr. "I will even give up my own room if necessary. I can always sleep with the servants in the attic."

Phoebe's lips twitched. "I'm sure that won't be necessary."

"She can have my room," Joshua offered from the stairs. "I can sleep practically anywhere. West always says so."

"We will put her in the blue room," Phoebe said firmly. "Next to Captain Parry and Eliza."

Deborah clapped her hands. "It's just like a house party. We shall have to play charades."

"Oh, yes, can I join in, too?" Joshua asked.

Phoebe bit her lips to keep from laughing, and Lady Amelia, who looked rather stunned, glanced uncertainly at Blackerby.

He leaned closer to whisper, "You see, with four dragons in the house, and everyone on guard against the Luddites, I could not leave you in safer—or more cheerful—company."

"Thank you," she muttered. Then she turned to Lady Westing. "Thank you so much for making room for me."

Lady Westing smiled sincerely. "As Deborah says, it will be like a house party. I only hope you will not find it trying on your nerves. At least your room will be quiet."

Lady Amelia smiled at that, and Blackerby felt assured that she would be well there.

She caught him with a look and a whispered word. "Thank you for rescuing me, my lord, but please know that I do not hold with any offers made under duress."

Despite expecting Lady Amelia to cry off, her words stung him more than he had foreseen.

He left the ladies with a bow and went to his next, much less pleasant appointment: reporting to the Prince Regent.

"He's in a foul mood," Farris warned him once they were back in the carriage.

"Naturally. I will do you a favor, Farris, and face Prinny alone. You may see if there's any sign of Randolph Blanchfield. Have someone watch his house, and his club and favorite gambling hells."

Farris nodded, though he looked dubious about his chances of success. "Good luck, my lord."

Blackerby would need it. No one had seen the Stone of Scone. No one had seen Randolph Blanchfield since he left his house the night of the fire. No one knew where Shaw was or what he planned next. And now, Blackerby was summoned to Carlton House to make an accounting to Prinny. Blackerby had been wholly invested for the last several hours in making certain Lady Amelia was safe, but the Prince Regent would hardly think that was a great accomplishment when the future of the nation hung in the balance.

Blackerby had his carriage deliver him to Pall Mall, and he stood before Carlton House. The great entrance with its Greek columns looked gray in the lingering fog and smoke from the fire. Blackerby even imagined he could still see drifts of smoke rising from the ruins of Westminster not far to the south. Perhaps the Prince Regent was right to take Blackerby to task this time. Blackerby was failing in his duty to protect England.

The red-coated Foot Guards didn't glance at Blackerby as he strode past—they were even well-trained enough not to flinch at his shadows —and the butler admitted Blackerby to His Highness's residence, his face giving away nothing of Prinny's mood that day. Blackerby kept his expression neutral, too, though Shade lashed his tail and the shadows swirled restlessly around Blackerby's feet.

Prinny summoned him into his chambers. The vaulted ceilings, richly colored draperies, and fresh gilding on the walls made it finer than the rooms the ill king occupied at St. James or the queen at Buckingham Palace. Two men stood guard by the door—Blackerby's own men. Even the Foot Guards might be bribed or blackmailed. Blackerby made certain his men would not be. They were those who had looked into the darkness and turned their back on it because they knew what terrors it held.

"Lord Blackerby," Prinny said, trying to cut Blackerby down a notch by studying him through a quizzing glass. It spoiled the effect that Prinny had to look up to see Blackerby.

"Your Highness." Very formal, the both of them. This did not bode well for the interview. Blackerby raised an eyebrow at Prinny's pristine white shirt. "I'm overjoyed to see that you don't let a little thing like rebellion ruin your sense of fashion. It wouldn't do to be caught dead with a wilting collar, now, would it?"

Prinny dropped his quizzing glass and glanced down at his clothes then at the shadows trailing along the floors of his chambers. They liked Carlton House. Full of secrets. The darkness whispered to Blackerby, echoes of past conversations too far faded to hear. But Blackerby detected the note of fear in them—fear emanating from the Prince Regent.

Prinny's dragon retreated from the shadows, keeping a wary eye on Shade, who made himself comfortable in the center of the rug.

"Can't you keep your entourage under control?" Prinny snapped.

"It is darkness, Your Highness. No one controls it."

"Yet it follows you around like you're the Prince of Darkness."

Blackerby's face stiffened at that. If it was the devil that Prinny wanted, it was the devil he would get. The always-hungry shadows slithered around him, and he let them seep into his skin, bringing their whispers with them. Whispers of the Prince Regent's secrets. His many sins, large and small, and his many insecurities. A self-indulgent prince who wanted crown and country, but not at the cost of his comfort. "They like me, Your Highness. And because they like me, they tell me things."

Blackerby's voice had a hiss to it. He was giving the darkness too much power. Too much control. It always wanted to control him. He pushed back, focusing on the dim light filtering in through the windows to warm his skin, and the shadows calmed and grew quiet.

Prinny had stepped away from Blackerby, his eyes wide. He cleared his throat and glanced down at the rings sparkling on his swollen finger. "Have they told you where we might find Shaw?"

Blackerby drew a slow breath. "Not yet, but I fancy we will find him in Scotland."

"Where he is fomenting further rebellion."

"That would be my guess," Blackerby said.

"I don't want your guesses!" Prinny snapped, dabbing his shiny forehead with his handkerchief. "I want my kingdom intact. I will not be like my father; I will not lose..." He swallowed hard. "Not lose any more of my empire."

Blackerby studied the Prince Regent. Was it the loss of colonies that Prinny feared or the loss of his senses? He glanced over at his men, who guarded Prinny's dragon from Shaw as much as they guarded the prince. Heavens knew that Prinny couldn't manage anything for himself.

Blackerby smirked at Prinny. "You focus on learning to tie that cravat correctly; I'll take care of the kingdom."

Prinny reddened. "Yes, you had better, or..." He trailed off and glanced at the guards.

What could he threaten? He wouldn't remove Blackerby. No matter how Blackerby had failed, no one else could do the job better. If Blackerby failed again—if Shaw succeeded—the Prince Regent would no longer have any power to threaten Blackerby. Blackerby would no longer have a kingdom to serve and protect. They both knew it.

"Don't fail me," Prinny said, his voice sounding like his cravat was too tight. "Don't fail England."

Blackerby pressed his lips together and fidgeted with his quizzing glass, tempted for a moment to level it at Prinny. To sneer at the Prince Regent's immaculate jacket and starched shirt collar: evidence that he had hidden inside while his city burned. He had magic, too—earth magic. True, the King's earth magic had failed against George Washington and his storm magic, but that had been over a great distance and against a land with its own dragons. The prince had never used his magic for anything but fortifying the foundations of his own building projects. Did a man who was not willing to sacrifice his own comforts and indulgences for his country really love it? Did he really deserve it?

But this was the burden Blackerby bore. He was the one who had to counter his own ties to the darkness regardless of what others did.

He slipped the quizzing glass back in his pocket and bowed.

Prinny dismissed him with a languid wave of his jeweled hand.

Blackerby returned to the street, inwardly seething. The time he wasted with Prinny could have been spent actually accomplishing something. He thought briefly of Amelia, wondering if she was comfortable, but he quickly pushed the thought aside. He couldn't afford to be distracted. Couldn't afford to make mistakes.

Farris caught up with him as he walked east, meeting Blackerby's long stride with his own brisk one.

"Any luck with Blanchfield?" Blackerby asked.

"None, sir. It's like he's vanished."

"More likely, he's gone to France to tattle on us to Napoleon. Confound him!"

"Or to Scotland with Shaw to put his own bony arse on the Stone of Scone," Farris suggested with a chuckle.

Blackerby stopped in his tracks, forcing a couple of gentlemen to stumble around him. One raised a fist as though he would challenge Blackerby, but then he noticed the shadows beginning to churn around them, and they kept their heads down and hurried on their way.

Blackerby tried to force his thoughts to settle, though he could almost hear the whispers of the shadows. They were laughing. "Put his own... Farris, how closely related are the Blanchfields to the royal family?"

"Their father's an earl. That's all I know."

Blackerby stared absently at the heavy grey clouds, trying to recall his own lineage. He'd never put much weight on it, not sharing the same level of family pride that most scions of noble families relished, but he seemed to recall quite a few royal names on his family tree. "Do they have any relation to the ancient kings of Scotland? Shaw doesn't as far as we know, but what about Randolph Blanchfield?"

"Probably. Most old, titled families do, don't they?" Farris looked at him, his forehead wrinkled in concern. "Why, my lord? What are you thinking?"

"I'm thinking that Shaw may have found himself a puppet king."

Chapter Twelve

AMELIA SETTLED into her room at the Westings' townhouse, inspecting the dressing table as Jane unpacked her trunk. Based on the crib in the corner and the pile of baby gowns and bonnets stacked on the chair by the window, they had put her into the still-unneeded nursery. It must have been the last available chamber in the crowded house.

Amelia had never enjoyed large house parties. Her family had attended a few while her parents were seeking a match for her brother, and the parties had always seemed so stiff and awkward.

Or perhaps it was Amelia who had always felt awkward.

She spent the first night at the Westings' house bivouacked in the room. Jane slipped out to eat with the servants and catch up on the gossip in a new house, but Amelia stared out her window at Berkeley Square below, not so different from Grosvenor Square. An ice shop sat on one corner instead of a coffee shop, but the same sorts of ladies and gentlemen strolled by, the same constant rumble of carriages overwhelmed any birds who sang in the trees. The fire had not stopped the *haut ton*'s social activities. If anything, the desire to gossip had intensified them. There was a sense of safety and solidarity in gathering in the face of terror—in sharing the burden. It made Amelia feel terribly lonely until she spotted her little street sweep in the square.

Blackerby had not forgotten her.

That was foolishness. Blackerby felt a sense of responsibility to keep her safe. He had only pretended to wish to marry her to save her from her father's wrath and give himself an excuse to take her to the Westings. To lock her in yet another modern castle where she would be out of the way. It seemed to be all she was good at—staying unseen. If only someone would see her. But perhaps she wasn't worthy of notice.

With those lowering thoughts, she curled up to feign sleep before Jane came back upstairs.

Amelia eventually slept a little and woke feeling low. She passed the morning sketching in her little notebook, but she didn't want to be rude to her hosts, so she allowed Jane to help her change and went down for nuncheon rather than having a tray sent to her room.

Lord Westing stood outside the dining room like a soldier at attention, his perpetual scowl softened only a little when he glanced across the room at his wife. His dragon sat on his shoulder, its tail lashing slowly, while Phoebe's dragon, Mushroom, sniffed at the dishes on the side table.

Westing bowed to Amelia. "I'm glad to have you here with us, Lady Amelia." His voice was cool, but his eyes were sincere. Not so cold beneath the surface.

"I fear I have caused you a great deal of trouble, and I am sorry for it," Amelia said.

"Not at all. The trouble is of Shaw's making, and we are glad to have our friends and allies gathered together." And he actually smiled, crumbling his icy demeanor.

Amelia returned the smile, but she caught Eliza watching her, her eyes narrowed in suspicion. Eliza's purple dragon lashed its tail, and Eliza ran her finger along the rim of her glass, causing the water inside to form a tiny whirlpool. Amelia glanced down. The two women had never been friendly, but Eliza's speculative glare made Amelia's stomach tighten. Did Eliza know her secret? If so, why not just reveal her?

She was glad to be seated between Lord Westing and Max Hart at supper, with Phoebe across from her. She and Eliza could ignore each other. Deborah, though, didn't hesitate to lean across Max to speak to Amelia as the footman brought around roast chicken.

"So, it *was* my uncle who burned Parliament?" Deborah asked, her eyes glittering with rage. "I wish I were the one who uncovered his secrets. I know I must face my uncle to avenge my family's name and honor, even if it costs me my life," she added in a melancholy tone.

Amelia sipped her wine to avoid smiling then said, "Miss Shaw, I'm certain it need not cost you anything. Certainly, you have already done as much as anyone could expect against your uncle."

"Yes, exactly!" Max said, patting Deborah's hand. "Thank you, Lady Amelia. That is just what I've been telling her. Nothing to blame Deb—Miss Shaw for."

"Oh, Mr. Hart," Deborah sighed, lowering her eyelashes prettily. "You are so sweet, but you cannot know what it is to have a sullied family name."

"I believe our honor rests in our actions and not in our family names," Amelia said.

Deborah's mood lightened instantly, and she grinned. "You are quoting Miss Charity! I adore her books."

Amelia hadn't realized she was quoting herself. It was probably good that she did not speak to many members of Society, since she was sure to have given herself away. She noticed Eliza's sour expression. Ah, yes, Eliza's character in Miss Charity was a silly one. Well, Eliza was one of those people who glided through Society with her wealth and her dragon, taking no thought for anything but fashion and parties.

Deborah turned to Phoebe. "We can do charades this afternoon, can we not? Act out scenes from Miss Charity's books?"

Phoebe cast a quick look at Eliza's frown. "Some music might be in order."

"Capital idea, Phoebs," Max said quickly. "I have missed your singing, Miss Shaw."

Deborah's scowl disappeared, and she beamed at Max.

The conversation continued on light, pleasant topics, and Amelia relaxed and enjoyed her nuncheon. Perhaps the problem had not been house parties. Perhaps it had been the company.

Though, as she thought of company, she realized she was the only unattached lady there. True, Deborah and Max were not officially engaged, but she suspected their relatively young ages were the only thing holding them back. It left her feeling lonely. Her situation had not changed but seeing the happiness around her made her more aware of it. And it seemed impossible that her situation would change after having remained the same for so long. The thought dulled her appetite, and when Phoebe prevailed upon Lord Westing to produce strawberry sorbet—cooled with his ice magic, of course—Amelia had to force herself to eat it, hardly tasting the cold, sweet-and-tangy treat as it melted on her tongue.

After nuncheon, they retreated to the drawing room for music. It was gloomy outside, but Phoebe played first, conjuring lights to dance around the room as she performed. The lights took the form of dancing couples, and everyone applauded enthusiastically at the end.

Amelia found herself missing her harp, even with all the tuning, as she was never more than passable at the pianoforte. She remembered how Lord Blackerby's eyes had sparkled when she played the chords wrong.

"Lady Amelia?" Phoebe prompted. "Will you perform? You seem to have some pleasant song in mind."

"Oh!" Amelia blushed. "I will sing."

She had a respectable voice, but she soon learned it was not as sweet as Deborah's, nor as rich as Eliza's alto.

Captain Parry surprised Amelia by joining his wife in a song of the sea. The way they looked at each other, Amelia imagined the recently married couple would have preferred not to have been at a crowded house party. Eliza and Parry didn't have to stay where Shaw might harm them. They didn't have estates to manage or roles in Parliament. They chose to stay and fight Shaw's Luddites.

Phoebe clapped enthusiastically for their performance. Eliza bowed and smiled at her friend, though her eyes betrayed her concern for Phoebe.

Captain Parry showed Eliza to a chair near Amelia, then went to fetch his wife a drink as Deborah coaxed Max into singing with her.

Amelia glanced at Eliza and whispered, "It is good of you to stay here to protect Lady Westing."

Eliza raised an eyebrow. "What makes you think that's why I'm here? I would miss London if I left. There's so much shopping."

Eliza might not know Amelia was Miss Charity, but she obviously sensed Amelia's opinion about her.

Amelia gave her a sad, half-smile. "You would not be willing to fight—to risk yourself—for Bond Street."

"Perhaps. Perhaps not." Eliza shrugged one shoulder. Then she smiled slightly. "There are some excellent shops."

Amelia smiled in return and turned her attention back to Max Hart and Deborah Shaw. She had thought Eliza an empty-headed lady addicted to shopping, but she had been wrong. She had been wrong to judge so many people. But it had seemed to be her path to freedom. What did that leave her now? The room took on a dimmer tone, the candles not as bright as they had been a moment before.

Deborah suddenly stopped singing, and her eyes widened. Amelia realized the room really had grown darker.

Everyone turned to find Lord Blackerby standing in the doorway with a timid-looking, bespectacled man hanging behind him. Blackerby bowed and gracefully draped himself into one of the chairs. "Oh, don't let me interrupt your little party. How jolly you all seem."

Amelia gave a guilty start. She had almost forgotten that the city was practically at war. She turned to Blackerby, hoping for some laughing glance from him, but he did not single her out. Why had she expected him to?

Deborah's face twisted up as if she would cry. "Oh, you are right! It is wicked of us to enjoy ourselves while my uncle is out there."

"Not at all," Westing said, giving Blackerby a cold look. "As we are wiling away our time waiting for news, it is wise to keep our spirits up."

"You need wile no longer," Blackerby said, waving a languid hand at his companion. "This is Mr. Thayne, my dragon expert, and we have come to you with a problem. I think I can find no group better acquainted with Shaw and with dragons than this one, not to mention in possession of such a fine library."

"I'm listening," Westing said, though his voice held an edge of wariness.

"We are wondering," Thayne said, licking his lips nervously, "if chaos might be an element that a dragon could be linked to. It's a fascinating question, you see, because—"

"Tut-tut," Blackerby said. "Our friends need a little background information to know why it's not only fascinating, but pressingly pertinent." He turned to the others. "You are aware the Stone of Scone has been stolen from Westminster Abbey."

Everyone nodded. This was no longer news. Try as he might, Blackerby could not have kept it a secret.

Blackerby went on. "My first thought was that Shaw might be trying to create a breakaway kingdom. Still a possibility, but I have learned that ancient Scottish kings were believed to be able to control the chaos of the elements, and it seemed to be related to their being crowned upon the Stone of Scone."

After a short pause, Captain Parry asked, "Is chaos an element?"

Phoebe gasped. "If it is an element that can be dragon-linked, the stone might be the dragon's object."

"Precisely." Blackerby smiled at her in an approving way that Amelia was surprised to find she was jealous of.

Amelia wasn't going to fade into the background of this conversation. "Shaw might be planning to destroy the dragon it's linked to instead of controlling it. Isn't that what happened in Dorset?"

Blackerby turned his wicked-sharp eyes on her now, and she thought she detected a gleam of approbation in them. "Exactly my question. One of them, at least. First, I need to know if there is a dragon attuned to chaos. Then, I need to know what Shaw would like to do with it."

Amelia shivered at the thought.

"For the first question," Blackerby went on, "I bring Mr. Thayne into the discussion. Now, Thayne, I drop the reins and give you your head."

Thayne grinned at that. "Thank you, my lord! I have long

suspected that there may be elements that people are attuned to that we haven't realized yet. Dragon magic clearly goes beyond the basics of earth, wind, fire, and water. Darkness and light, hot and cold, why not creation and destruction—order and chaos, in other words? Those are also natural forces in the world. I know several scientists who are studying the way natural systems have a tendency to break apart over time..." He seemed to realize that he was losing his audience, and he cleared his throat. "Well, you see, I don't think the idea of a chaos dragon is out of the question."

"Good heavens!" Phoebe exclaimed. "To think of such a creature in the hands of someone like Shaw."

"But if such a dragon exists," Westing said, "Why have we not heard of it?"

"Because it has been sleeping for hundreds of years," Blackerby said. "The stone may have given the ancient kings some link to the slumbering chaos dragon in the way that Mrs. Parry was able to contact the water dragon, but since Edward Longshanks took the stone to England centuries ago, it's been used as a symbol of dominance rather than a magical tool. Shaw may hope to change that. Throw our nation into further chaos. Or, alternatively, he might see some advantage in destroying the chaos dragon."

"Destroying destruction," Amelia said. "How would he benefit?"

"Chaos, destruction, they are necessary for change," Thayne said. "For new growth. Imagine if things stayed exactly as they are. A mad king. A Prince Regent who is—" He looked guilty for a moment and said carefully, "Who is not always well liked. Napoleon triumphant on the continent. Think of what the water and storm dragons did for us against the Spanish Armada. What if the chaos dragon had a hand, er, talon, whatever... in it as well? We might atrophy."

"Whichever is the most likely possibility," Blackerby said, "I want to know if it's possible. If Shaw could do it. I hoped, Westing, we might have access to your library. It is the only link we have to any information about the use of a dragon's elemental objects in trying to harm or control them."

"Of course," Westing said, his voice weary.

Phoebe stood a little awkwardly, hand on her belly. "I don't understand why Shaw doesn't just find the White Dragon's object and destroy that. I'm sure he'd like to."

"No doubt, but no one knows where or even what it is," Thayne said.

"And we want to keep it that way," Blackerby added, a warning note in his voice.

Something else troubled Amelia. "But, if the stone is supposed to be the object of a chaos dragon, wouldn't it be less...ordinary?"

Thayne looked ready to pounce on that question, but Blackerby grinned and answered first. "There are reasons to believe it only looks ordinary because it wishes to. Or because the dragon wishes it to. You see, old stories describe the stone in a variety of ways: black basalt, white marble, words etched on it. If there were just one variation, I would think Edward Longshanks simply stole the wrong stone. But with so many variations, I began to wonder if the stone itself didn't change over time."

A cold chill ran down Amelia's back. "If there is a chaos dragon, and it's still aware and controlling the stone—"

Blackerby nodded and finished her thought. "Then it may be using Shaw as much as Shaw is using it. It would want chaos, and Shaw could give it its heart's desire."

Westing took his wife's arm. "We had best get started, then."

He led the way into the large library, the shelves filled with books. Amelia felt a twinge of guilt seeing her own books on those shelves, but Westing gestured to a group of ancient-looking volumes.

"I collected all the books related to dragons here, including my family's accounts."

Amelia recalled at the house party in Lyme Regis when her hostess had revealed that the Westing ancestors had killed a great dragon. Apparently, Westing had been preparing to make sure it wouldn't happen again.

"Do you think," Phoebe asked, lifting one of the books, "that breaking the stone might destroy the dragon's power?"

"I don't know," Westing said. "The Dorset Dragon's ring wasn't broken. It's more like its power was broken. I think it has to do with how they tried to use the ring. Mrs. Parry was able to use the water dragon's jewel without harming it."

"By working with it," Eliza said, looking thoughtful and worried.

"Then the danger to the dragon is in a struggle of wills between the dragon and the holder of the object?" Amelia suggested.

Blackerby straightened. "That could be. But it doesn't help us with Shaw. We are assuming the dragon would want the kind of chaos he proposes to bring about."

"Have you ever investigated Shaw's background?" Westing asked. "Tried to find out where he came from? What drives him?"

"Of course, but even with the information Miss Shaw gave us, there is little to be found. They are of an old, respectable family, I understand, but it seems this most recent generation has gone to ground and erased their trail. We did find a record of an Archibald Shaw petitioning against a certain Lord Whitson's enclosure of public lands. That Shaw was a local squire and may have been the current Shaw's father, but the trail goes cold after there."

"That would have been my grandfather, then?" Deborah looked keenly interested. "Did he win his case?"

"I don't believe any action was taken to stop Lord Whitson. It's difficult to say because the records are scattered and not always complete. I have not found anyone with memory of the people involved. Shaw remains an enigma."

Westing glowered at that, and Phoebe bit her lip. Yes, bad news all around.

Amelia's eyes brightened. "What if we could find a great dragon willing to help us?"

Blackerby looked to Thayne, who nodded.

"It's certainly possible. I don't know if an ancient dragon would fight for us, but it might give us information. We would have a better chance if the person trying to contact the dragon was attuned to the same ability."

Blackerby lips curled up. "The Red Dragon of Wales has been friendly to humans in the past. It is attuned to fire. I wonder if Mrs. Reynolds of Bond Street might fancy a journey west."

"And what of the White Dragon under the Tower?" Westing asked.

Thayne tapped his chin. "Legend states that it would help defend England in a time of great need. It's so old and retiring that we don't know much about it. We're not even certain what it's attuned to, but our best guess is earth."

"Like the Prince Regent," Phoebe said brightly.

Blackerby's mouth twitched in what Amelia thought was dislike. "We will want to keep our future monarch out of the fray if it comes to a fight."

"But Eliza could bring the water dragon!" Phoebe looked so excited, Amelia wondered if she wanted a battle against Shaw. "Is there a light dragon somewhere?" Her dragon hissed. "Oh, don't worry, Mushroom, it could never replace you. I only want to help."

Amelia wished she could help, but she was once again on the outside, a dancer seated by the wall watching others swirl past.

Blackerby nodded. "Perhaps. It is worth looking into. We have mostly left the great dragons alone, assuming that is what they desire, but I cannot imagine they would want the Luddites to win."

An urgent pounding at the outside door brought everyone's attention around, and the butler entered with Farris at his heels.

"My lord," Farris huffed, trying to catch his breath. "There has been an assassination attempt on the Prince Regent. Shot at in Hyde Park."

Chapter Thirteen

BLACKERBY SENSED a quiver of excitement run through the shadows at news of the attack on the Prince Regent. Would darkness prefer chaos over order? Would his own magic betray him in this fight?

"That block-headed idiot," Blackerby said, earning a shocked look from Mr. Thayne. "What was he doing in the Park?"

Farris shuffled his feet. "Apparently, he thought it would be good for morale."

"Oh, yes, a dead prince always cheers the masses."

In fact, some of them would be happy to have Prinny gone, but it would not benefit the kingdom, not when the prince's brother, the Duke of York, was only a shade less scandalous, and Princess Charlotte, though popular, was not yet twenty and would be rather young to fill in as a Princess Regent. No, the loss of the Prince Regent would tip the country into perilous waters.

And everyone was looking to Blackerby now, wondering what he would do about it. He met Lady Amelia's eyes, and the confidence he saw there first warmed him, then made him feel guilty. He didn't have the answer.

"Have you made His Highness safe?" Blackerby asked Farris.

"Yes, my lord. He is locked down in Carlton House."

"As soon as practical, I want him moved to St. James Palace. It's more secure." Blackerby drew a deep breath. "Was anyone injured?"

"A member of the Foot Guards. A bullet grazed his arm. He's likely to recover. His Highness bore it with remarkable calm," Farris said, gulping in another huge breath of air. "He said that the man must be mad and shouldn't be hurt. They're holding him—"

"They caught the villain, then?" Westing asked, looking like he wanted to go several bouts with the would-be assassin in the ring.

"Was it my uncle?" Deborah asked.

Farris looked between them, trying to answer everyone at once. "The park was crowded. He couldn't escape. He appeared to be a well-born, respectable gentleman, but no one seems to know who he is."

"A Luddite, if I'm not mistaken." Blackerby glanced at the others in the room, who were watching with wide eyes. "Shaw is good at disguises, though. Miss Shaw, I will ask you to try to identify the man from your time among the Luddites." He glanced at Amelia, who had gone especially pale. "Lady Amelia, you mentioned interrupting the meeting of a lady and a gentleman in the library, and at the same time that my informants suspected a meeting between Luddites was taking place. I wonder if you might have seen some of the conspirators after all."

"But the men with the petition…"

Farris cleared his throat. "My lord, this man had a petition with him."

Blackerby gritted his teeth. "An imitator, then? Or confederates?" He looked again to Lady Amelia. "You saw the last person—a gentleman?"

"Well, he looked like one, but now I have my doubts."

"So do I, my dear lady. I would like you to come with me as well, if you would. You and Miss Shaw may help us untangle this conspiracy."

Lady Amelia nodded, her face brightening, and Blackerby was surprised at how much that buoyed him. He should not ever count on help from anyone, but something about Amelia's no-nonsense presence made her feel like a partner he could rely on.

Farris shifted from foot to foot. "The House of Commons wished to meet immediately. Since Westminster is in ruins, the queen offered them the use of Buckingham Palace. They complained that it was shabby, but they accepted."

Lady Westing's eyes widened at that. Clearly, the place had made an impression on her, but the members of Parliament were difficult to please. They hadn't liked Westminster, either, before it had gone up in flames, but nostalgia made everything brighter.

"By all means," Blackerby said, "they will need to meet. The House of Lords, too." A thought stopped him. "But let them know they are not to meet in the same place or at the same time. We are lucky enough that Westminster was only incidental to their real goal, or the Luddites might have crippled our entire government."

Farris nodded, and Blackerby motioned for Miss Shaw and Lady Amelia to join him. "Come, ladies. Accompany me for a stroll in the Park."

Amelia hurried along with Blackerby and Deborah Shaw. Deborah's eyes gleamed with excitement and anger. Amelia had never included Deborah in her books because she wasn't sure what to make of the girl or where she fit in the scheme of things: not noble or common, dragon-linked but Luddite-raised, and dramatic enough in person that perhaps she didn't need a role in a novel.

Blackerby said little as they rushed through the crowds, but his mouth was set in a determined frown. The people Amelia brushed past were not the usual crush of carriage, shoppers, merchants, and pickpockets, but knots of people huddled in worried talk or loudly crowing dire predictions of England falling as France had. The energy was different. Wrong. Amelia could taste the tension, something metallic. Like blood.

She caught another glimpse of Blackerby's fierce expression and quickened her step so she wouldn't fall behind. Blackerby had singled her out to help him. She could not let him down.

They entered Hyde Park, where the usual parade had ground to a standstill, all attention focused toward the Serpentine. The lake's waters rippled dully, reflecting the ashen sky. As always, the crowd parted for Blackerby, a proverbial Moses among the sea of onlookers. He stopped before a pair of Foot Guards holding a man under arrest.

"Is the Prince Regent secure?" Blackerby asked, his voice carrying over the murmurs of the crowd.

"He's at Carlton House, my lord," one of the Foot Guards said.

"I want him at St. James Palace."

The Foot Guards exchanged an uncomfortable look. "He doesn't want to go there. Says it's like a dungeon."

Blackerby leaned closer to the nearest guard, keeping his voice low enough that it didn't reach the interested onlookers. "Tell His Highness that I will put him in a dungeon if that's what it takes to keep him safe. This is not about him. It's about England."

The guard nodded, eyes wide. "I will convey the message."

"As long as you also convey His Highness to safety. And I want the Duke of York and Princess Charlotte out of the city." Blackerby raised his voice again. "Now, about the prisoner."

The guard gestured to the man they held down.

Blackerby approached him, and the shadows billowed around him, reaching out like tentacles. Several of the Foot Guards winced, and Amelia restrained herself from rolling her eyes. Hadn't they realized yet that shadows couldn't hurt them?

Blackerby's dragon, perched on his shoulder, extended his wings, giving Blackerby the look of an avenging angel. The would-be assassin quailed before him. Amelia felt a little sorry for the man, especially recognizing as she did that Blackerby was putting on a show to frighten him. But then she remembered that this man was a conspirator who wished to take down the nation.

Blackerby gestured for the guards to bring the man closer. The prisoner struggled a little but grew still and wide-eyed as they shuffled him nearer to Blackerby, within the orbit of the shadows. They swirled around the man then settled at Blackerby's feet. Blackerby put on his charming but sardonic smile. It gave Amelia an odd feeling, like she was watching an actor at work.

"Now, Mr....?" Blackerby said.

The man lifted his chin. "You may call me Mr. Smith."

One side of Blackerby's lips curled up. "Mr. Smith, then. What was the meaning of your actions here today?"

"I come bearing a message: Change is coming."

"You realize you are in a great deal of trouble?"

The prisoner glared at Blackerby, and his eyes flicked to Deborah Shaw with her pale-yellow dragon perched on her shoulder. "It is not I who is in trouble, but you and all the other dragon-linked."

"Are we, though? I doubt it. You and your friend Shaw are not clever enough to best us."

The prisoner's eyes narrowed. Amelia silently applauded Blackerby. He had hit on the man's weak spot.

Mr. Smith sneered at him. "You have no idea whom you're dealing with. Shaw will usher in an age of freedom and equity for all—not just those who have a dragon."

Amelia shifted. It sounded like a noble idea. No one pushed to the margins because she didn't have a dragon. No one bound by the archaic expectations of a decaying social order. But even if Amelia believed Shaw could bring such a utopia about, she could not approve of his methods.

"And Shaw will be more equal than the rest, I imagine," Blackerby said, drawing his quizzing glass and leveling it at the man. "Was that what he promised you, too? I suppose you're hoping he will free you from prison when he rises to power."

"It doesn't matter," the man said, shrugging one shoulder. "The important thing is that those like you will no longer be in a position to prey on those like me."

Blackerby smiled sadly and twirled the quizzing glass. "No, you would see different people in power to prey on different people in a position of weakness. Have you heard the stories coming out of France? Power corrupts, my dear. It turns men into animals."

The man snarled and tried to tear his arms free to lash at Blackerby.

"Precisely." Blackerby pocketed his quizzing glass and made a shooing motion to the guards. "You may take him away."

"Your blood will run in the streets!" Mr. Smith shouted as the guards hauled him off.

Blackerby sighed heavily, and Amelia saw true sadness in his expression.

Blackerby motioned for her and Deborah to walk away with him. Amelia felt the weight of many gazes on their backs.

"Did you know him, Miss Shaw?" he asked Deborah in a low voice.

She shook her head. "He must be one of the newer members of my uncle's group."

"More fool he, then," Blackerby said.

Deborah nodded. "Where are we going now?"

"We go to Buckingham Palace. The House of Commons is assembling today, and I want to be certain there is no trouble there. Keep your eyes sharp."

Deborah nodded and marched forward, a little ahead of them. Amelia almost believed that Blackerby was deliberately falling behind to walk with her.

"I thought you said the Lords must stay away from the House of Commons," Amelia said to him.

One corner of his mouth twitched. "But I am not just any lord. Surely, you've realized that by now."

"Yes," Amelia snapped. "You are a very foolish one sometimes. What's to stop an assassin from shooting at *you*?"

Blackerby stopped and cocked his head to study her. "Why, my dear, I would almost think you're concerned for me. Certainly, my death would free you from an inconvenient engagement?"

Amelia's cheeks burned, but she rallied. "Are you suggesting you would rather die than see it through?"

"Not at all," he murmured, lifting a finger to brush a strand of hair from her face, then tracing a gentle line along her jaw.

Amelia stared at him, her pulse humming as his touch—and his gaze—lingered near her lips.

He drew an unsteady breath and slowly pulled his hand away, clenching it into a fist. "But, alas, I have other responsibilities besides amusing pretty redheads. This—" He gestured around the Park full of gossiping knots of ladies and gentlemen— "is what I was born to do."

"Is it?" Amelia asked, without thinking. Blackerby gave her a curious look, and she pressed on. "You think you were born to be the Home Secretary?"

He took her arm, guiding her forward. "I was born to darkness. Managing spies and ruffians is one of the few honorable courses open to me."

Amelia thought of her own family's legacy of decaying gentility. "Legacies are a hard burden to carry. But I wonder if you're seeing yours wrong."

"Oh?" He sounded indifferent, but Amelia didn't believe the act.

"Just because you're attuned to darkness doesn't mean it's a part of you—any more than it's a part of any of us. You just understand it better than most."

His forehead creased as if he were considering her words. "Ah, but there's something you don't know—no one does." He kept his voice low, so she had to walk closer to hear. Close enough that her arm brushed his, and his scent of sandalwood reached her. "It's not just that the shadows whisper secrets to me. They want more—they want to crawl inside of me. To make me part of them. I'm not aware of any other element that does the same."

Amelia was silent as she digested that. "You do carry a terrible burden. But that doesn't mean you're destined to lose yourself to the darkness. It might mean you were born with the strength to fight it."

He raised an eyebrow, and the shadows swirled up around them like sediment disturbed by a stone's throw. He brushed his hands through them. "Shadow isn't something you can fight. It has no substance."

"But it flees the light. Maybe that's the point—to shine light into the darkness and disperse it."

"I am not attuned to light."

"And those who are, I've observed, seem rather ignorant of the darkness. They live in the brightness of the moment, cheerful and somewhat ignorant."

"Like Lady Westing." He paused. "Or Lady Millicent?"

"You don't know her, my lord. Many others would have become sour in such circumstances. She is sharp, but she retains an optimism I have to admire. But neither of those ladies understand darkness well enough to fight it."

"Hmm." Blackerby stared ahead, his brow furrowed in thought.

Amelia had to repress an urge to reach out and try to soothe those worries, to reassure Blackerby that she saw more in him than the darkness that troubled him. She blushed at the audacity of her imagination, though. Blackerby didn't need her words of comfort. She had nothing to offer him.

Chapter Fourteen

BUCKINGHAM PALACE TOOK shape out of the smoky fog hanging over the city. Blackerby scanned every sculpted shrub and hedge in the gardens for possible threats. The shadows were active, anxious. He couldn't be sure if they were reacting to a gloomy day or their excitement over Shaw's schemes.

Miss Shaw strode ahead, her fists curled and her dragon riding the currents overhead, but Lady Amelia's steps were heavy. The shadows whispered to him of pain and heartache—as certain a form of darkness as he had ever seen, but one he did not know how to fight, except by sarcasm and indifference. He was not such a dolt to think that either would be of use to Lady Amelia at the moment.

Blackerby remembered what Amelia had said about love dying one piece at a time. He had thought she spoke only of romantic love, but the shadows whispered to him that it was something more. Children loved their parents, yet what happened to that adoration as a parent daily, monthly, yearly made stinging comments that rubbed the child's heart until it was bleeding and raw? The light of filial adoration would fade and finally flicker to darkness. And what of the love between childhood friends? The innocent affection of youth could be rooted deep, and when it was plucked out bit by bit as one watched a friend drift into selfishness or meanness, the wounds would also cut deep into the flesh of the heart.

Yet Blackerby was no physician. His magic was for hearing secrets and seeing into dark places. He tried to prevent the hurts from happening, but he had no gift for healing them.

They reached the long wings of Buckingham Palace. Members of the House of Commons milled about in front of the queen's residence. The queen would have been removed to St. James with her ill husband and contrary son. Just in case. The Foot Guard patrolled the grounds of the palace, London constables held back the mass of watching people, and some of Blackerby's Runners mingled with the crowd.

Blackerby strode forward, taking for granted that people would move for him. And they did, allowing him to guide Lady Amelia and Miss Shaw up to where the Prime Minister, Spencer Perceval, was talking to one of the guards admitting people to the palace. Blackerby stopped, watching the crowd for any disturbance. Amelia and Miss Shaw studied the people around them. The impatient faces of the members of Parliament, anxious with worry for the nation, crowded close. Many of them were dragon-linked as well or had family members who were. They wanted to be in the palace, where they hoped to be safe, and they wanted to be acting instead of waiting. Blackerby did, too. He took out his quizzing glass and spun it on its chain.

"Wait!" one of the constables called.

Everyone turned to look. A tall man had pushed past the constable. The tall man looked around, as if uncertain what to do once he was past the human barricade. Blackerby tightened his grip on the quizzing glass, the metal frame biting into his palm. He stepped forward, getting ready to summon his Runners.

But he glanced at Amelia. Her attention was elsewhere. On a woman clutching a baby wrapped in a blanket. A woman who had slipped past the guards while they were distracted.

Amelia's face went white, and she started toward the woman, glancing back with panic in her eyes.

Her gaze met Blackerby's, and he understood. She recognized the woman.

Shade hissed. Blackerby broke into a run.

Amelia shouted something at the woman. "Stop," perhaps. Her voice came out raspy, winded.

"Stop!" Blackerby echoed her call.

He overtook Lady Amelia, putting himself between her and the woman with the baby.

"Stop her!" Blackerby gestured at the woman.

His Runners, confused for a moment, caught on and turned to capture her.

But the woman let her blanket fall, revealing a doll and a dueling pistol. The doll fell to the ground, its glassy, dead eyes staring at the gray sky. The woman raised the pistol. The Runners were too far. Blackerby was too far. Amelia managed a hoarse scream. The members of Parliament looked around in confusion, and a Foot Guard noticed the woman. He stared for a moment, frozen, then leaped forward.

The pistol flashed. A bright blast of light. Then came the thunderous report. The screams. One of the Runners tackled the woman.

The prime minister staggered back, clutching his chest.

Blackerby stumbled to a stop, his throat tight. Shade jumped onto his shoulder as if about to use it to launch himself into the air, but he stopped there, wings outstretched in uncertainty.

Blackerby pivoted and ran toward the prime minister. He mindlessly barked orders to the guards, to the crowd, even to the prime minister. But Spencer Perceval didn't respond. Couldn't.

The prime minister gasped, "Murder." Then his mouth moved soundlessly, and he stared at the blood on his hand, seeping over his waistcoat.

Blackerby caught Perceval as he slumped to the ground. "He still has a pulse." He pointed to a Foot Guard. "You! Get me a surgeon!"

Perceval's body was limp, his skin growing paler as the blood soaked through his shirt.

One of the members of Parliament rushed up to Blackerby. "I'm a physician. Let me attend him."

Blackerby stepped back, holding his bloodied hands away from his coat. Farris handed him a handkerchief.

The physician pressed on Perceval's wound, felt his throat for a pulse, then shook his head. "He's gone."

Beside Blackerby, Amelia gasped and covered her mouth.

The Luddites had assassinated the prime minister.

Blackerby looked at the men gathered around him, beckoning those Runners who seemed most composed. "Go. Make certain the Prince Regent is safe. Put him under double guard immediately. Keep him apart from the cabinet and members of Parliament. This might not be the last assassin."

His Runners dispersed like smoke, and the gathered members of Parliament, suddenly understanding the situation, began to take themselves off. Good. Blackerby didn't have the resources to protect all of them. They would have to protect themselves.

He felt cold and numb, like the shadows had wormed their way inside of him. Everything was falling apart, and he could only catch at threads. The shadows coiled around his legs, whispering to him. Taunting him with his failures. If he let the darkness in, it promised to make him stronger, smarter. He crumpled the bloodied handkerchief and tossed it to the ground.

Deborah Shaw stared wide-eyed at the fallen prime minister, her face linen-white, and her pale lips moving soundlessly. Her dragon flapped in agitation, and thunder rumbled somewhere above the smoky haze. They could not afford Miss Shaw's hysterics at the moment.

Blackerby motioned for Farris. "Escort Miss Shaw away. Find her a carriage." He pointed to the physician. "Move Perceval's body to Downing Street. Notify the coroner. We'll need to hold an inquest. Confound it. He has a wife. Children?"

"Twelve, my lord," one of the guards muttered.

Blackerby pressed his eyes shut so tightly that he saw flashes of color in the darkness. "We will be sure the government provides for them. In the meantime, I need to know what happened here."

"The woman's not speaking," the guard said to Blackerby.

Blackerby waved him off. "We hardly need her to. She's acting for Shaw. He's the one we need to find."

He paced, Shade clinging to his back. The Prince Regent was locked down under guard—he hoped—and soon the members of Parliament and the king's cabinet would be as well. He had to focus on Shaw.

"It's my fault," Amelia mumbled.

"What?" Blackerby asked more sharply than he meant to.

She jumped. "We thought the men at the party were using papers to hide a weapon, and then they used the same trick to get close to the Prince Regent and the prime minister."

Blackerby sighed. "Perhaps. They might have been testing the idea out at the party. We cannot know, and there is no reason to torment ourselves with doubts. No, we need to move forward. Shaw is not the weak link in the chain. Help me find the Blanchfield siblings."

Amelia stared at him. "You cannot really believe Millicent is involved."

Blackerby hesitated, knowing he was delivering bad news, but Lady Amelia needed to know. "Lord and Lady Greenley wish to keep it quiet, but she is missing. In fact, you may have been the last person to see her."

She gripped her hands together. "Why didn't you tell me?"

"I have been a bit too busy to keep you up to date with every on-dit, my dear. And I only recently found out myself. Now, where might I find her?"

"Pierre Moreau has probably kidnapped her! She must be in terrible danger."

"Hmph. Unless he drugged her dragon, it would be difficult for Moreau to take her unwillingly."

Her eyes narrowed. "You think she went with him. How can you think so badly of everyone?"

"Because the darkness shows me their bad sides. Loyalty to your friends is admirable, but you are not a foolish hopeful like Phoebe Westing. You know how to be realistic."

"Phoebe Westing is not foolish. And I don't drop my loyalty as easily as all that. Moreau may have tricked Millicent into going with him, but I believe her to be in danger. Perhaps you would see that, too, if you stopped reveling in the darkness."

Blackerby scowled at the accusation in her voice. "I don't have time for this. If she's in danger, help me find her."

She looked stung but gave him a defiant glare. "The family has a hunting box in Essex. It would be a good place to lie low."

"Excellent. I will send my men to check there for the Blanchfields."

"And Moreau." She said it in that wooden voice of hers that she sometimes used. In fact, Blackerby had noticed that when she reverted to that voice, she did not ask questions, merely stated what she saw as facts, as though she did not expect anyone to answer her. As if another part of her heart had died. He felt a twinge of guilt, but he could not allow himself distractions, and she was becoming much too distracting.

Blackerby turned away from her. "I have already searched Moreau's apartments as well as the house he rented last Season. There is no sign of him, but his room has been turned over, as if he fled in a hurry."

"As if he had kidnapped someone."

"Or as if he was involved in a plot to overthrow the government and was afraid he might be caught," he almost snarled. "Even if your friend has been kidnapped, which I find quite unlikely, my focus has to be on finding Shaw. You cannot expect me to put aside important matters for your whims."

She paled a bit, and he regretted his sharp tongue, but she needed to understand that he could never allow his personal interests to come first. That was the price he paid for being what he was. It was better that she knew that. That she not pin any false hopes on him.

"I see," she finally said. "Then it is up to me to find the truth."

Blackerby groaned inwardly. "I will not allow you to put yourself in danger. I will send you back to Berkeley Square with Miss Shaw, and Farris will make certain you stay there."

Farris, who had returned from finding a carriage, looked unhappy at this order, but Blackerby couldn't allow Lady Amelia to worry him. If she was locked in with the Westings, she would be safe, and whatever Lady Millicent had brought on herself, she could deal with the consequences.

Chapter Fifteen

Amelia retreated to her room at the Westings' townhouse. Fortunately, Deborah was happy to reenact the events of the day for everyone, and they could assume Amelia was too overwhelmed to talk about it. They didn't have to know Blackerby had anything to do with it.

She shouldn't have been surprised that he'd dismissed her. Had she really expected him to—what? Want to keep her around? Not when she wasn't useful to him. She was fortunate the Westings were willing to have her there.

She stared out the window. No sign of the little street sweep. Her window faced in the general direction of her home at Grosvenor Square, though the hazy air didn't allow her to see very far. She didn't miss it. At least here, no one was cutting her down. But she didn't know where she would go next.

Jane's footsteps echoed in the corridor outside the door, and Amelia curled up around the ache in her chest and pretended to be asleep. Her mind reviewed Blackerby's tone, the coldness in his eyes. She squeezed her eyes tighter, but then she saw the prime minister. His stunned expression as he sank to the ground. And Millicent's shining eyes when she talked about Pierre Moreau. What if Millicent really was guilty? Amelia had watched her change over the years, and not for the better. She might have lost her friend completely now.

It was many hours before she actually slept.

She woke to the late morning light, feeling heavy and achy. Jane was already out of the room, so Amelia stretched and cleaned her face in the cold water on the dressing table. She had let Blackerby's dismissal hurt her, but she couldn't dwell on that. She needed to think of how she could find the truth about Millicent.

She went down to breakfast, wondering if there was a way to trace Millicent by her dragon. When she walked into the dining room, all conversation stopped, and the company assembled there stared at her.

"What happened?" Amelia asked, her chest tightening. Had someone else been killed while she slept? Could she have done more to try to stop it?

Phoebe rose slowly from the table, putting on a nervous smile. "It is nothing to concern yourself with, dear. It's only... I'm afraid Shaw has found a new way to get revenge on you."

Amelia's thoughts went to her parents and her cousins, some of whom she was quite fond of. "Who?"

Phoebe shook her head and picked up a newspaper. "He hasn't physically harmed someone, but I suspect he is behind this."

Amelia's first thought was that her father had placed an announcement of her engagement to Blackerby in the newspapers. It would be like him, to make certain Amelia was really off of his hands. But certainly, that news couldn't seem so dreadful that it would fill Phoebe's eyes with fear.

Phoebe held the paper out. It wasn't turned to the first page—that must have all been news of the prime minister's assassination. But the bold headline struck Amelia like a blow to the chest.

Miss Charity Revealed
Lady Amelia Chase Tattling on the Beau Monde

Amelia didn't touch the paper. Didn't take it from Phoebe. She just stared at it, her mouth moving soundlessly as she tried to understand how her world had just been shattered.

"Don't worry, dear," Phoebe said. "No one who knows you will believe it. But you may be in for some difficult times."

Amelia wet her lips. "It wasn't Shaw. It was Randolph Blanchfield."

Deborah brightened. "Oh, is that who you were trying to help Lord Blackerby find?"

Amelia could only nod. Her throat felt gummy, like all her words were stuck in her gullet.

"Never liked him," Max said. "Something off about him."

"Well!" Phoebe said. "I can't say I ever liked him either, but to help the Luddites and then slander the name of his sister's friend! What a villain!"

"It's not slander." Amelia was surprised that the words were hers. She kept expecting someone else to say them, but when no one did, they forced their way from her lips.

Phoebe looked shocked for a moment, but then she smiled weakly. "Libel, then, not slander. Either way—"

"No," Amelia cut in. Phoebe was too kind, too good. She could not let them make excuses for her. She would not make them liars, too. "What I mean is—that headline is true. I wrote the Miss Charity books." She stared at the floor, unable to face anyone in that room. People she had deceived and mocked. "I was trying to make my own way... I didn't mean..."

It didn't matter. It didn't matter why she'd done it or how harmless she had thought it. She had hurt people. Hurt her friends. She had thought Society selfish, but she had been just as bad. Worse for being two-faced. She had longed to be loved and to be accepted, and when she wasn't, she had proven herself unworthy of either.

She couldn't stay. She couldn't face them. She felt the hurt and anger in the shocked silence, but she could not bring herself to see it in their eyes. Instead, she fled the room, barreling past Farris in the corridor.

"Lady Amelia!" Phoebe called.

Amelia pushed past the astonished butler and grasped the

doorknob. It was icy. She hissed at the sting of the cold metal against her skin but pulled it open, slamming it shut behind her just as the whole door froze solid under a layer of ice. She gasped at the sight, imagining how furious Lord Westing must be, then dashed down the front steps and out into the square. She wasn't afraid of assassins now. Randolph wasn't going to shoot at her. He didn't have to. She was already dead to Society. Ruined.

She was unused to running, but she put Berkeley Square far behind her before she had to stop and catch her breath. A few people gave her odd or curious looks. It would not take long for people to recognize her. Her blasted red hair. She needed to leave Mayfair.

Where could she go? Not home. She didn't have a home anymore. Her father would not accept her back. Not to her publisher. They never knew who she was before, but they would have nothing to do with her now that she was a pariah.

But her cousin Mrs. Jonston in Fleet Street would take her in. She would not approve of what Amelia had done, but she would not punish her more than what she was already suffering. And, while Amelia had left most of her savings behind at the Westings' house, she always carried some of it in the pocket hidden under her skirts. She could help her cousin. And when that ran out, she would…

What could she do? No one would hire a girl as a governess if they feared she might spy out their secrets and share them with the world. She would have to find shop work. Maybe Mrs. Reynolds would hire her.

What had she done?

As she started the long walk toward Fleet Street, keeping her face down and pulling her shawl over her hair, another thought stole the breath from her. Blackerby. He would truly have no use for her now that her secret was out. Not that he had much use for her before, but she would not be able to help him any longer. She would probably never see him again.

A hot tear spilled down her cheek, but she wiped it away with a vicious swipe. There would be no self-pity. She had brought this on herself, and she deserved it.

She blinked her eyes clear and hurried along. She passed the blackened ruins of Westminster, and another wave of guilt swept over her. She thought she was so observant, but what if she had actually had her eyes open? She might have realized Randolph was in trouble, going down a dark path. And Millicent. She might have done something to help her friend. In the future, she vowed to be as useful as her limited circle would allow, even if only to her cousin. She had to hope there was a future for England. Blackerby would see to that, though. Without her.

Cheapside greeted her with its loud bustle of merchants and shoppers. She relaxed a little. Here, she could be unknown.

A pair of women walked past. "Did you hear about Miss Charity?"

"Shocking!"

Amelia swallowed hard. Less known, anyway.

The bells of St. Paul's rang the hour, their somber tones echoing off the canyons of buildings. She passed the taverns and printing shops of Fleet Street and felt a thrill of excitement followed by another twinge of regret. She would not be writing anything serious now, either. At least, not under her own name. Perhaps she could use her cousins' name. There would be no danger of getting her into trouble, but Amelia would never write another scandalous word again. Maybe she would take up moralistic tales as penance.

She had almost reached her cousin's apartment above a popular pub. She climbed the stairs and glanced back over her shoulder. A familiar figure on the street below caught her eye. The woman wore a hooded cloak, but there could be no doubt it was Millicent Blanchfield.

Chapter Sixteen

MILLICENT BLANCHFIELD SNEAKING AROUND CHEAPSIDE? Something was definitely wrong. Amelia glanced at her cousin's worn, friendly door, then sighed and went back down the stairs to the crowded street.

It wasn't hard to find Millicent's hooded figure again. Millicent carried a basket over her arm like a shop girl, incongruous with her fine muslin dress. People coming and going from the nearby coffee shop gave her odd looks, and she adjusted the cloth covering the basket's contents. Someone caught her arm: a man lingering outside the coffee shop, a hat pulled low over his eyes.

Pierre Moreau.

Amelia stepped forward, ready to rescue her friend from the villain's clutches.

But Millicent smiled and extended her free hand to Pierre, who raised it to his lips. Millicent laughed, her voice trilling and her head thrown back for a moment, revealing a flash of white teeth. She did not look like a woman being held against her will.

She could still be a woman deceived—one so desperate for love that she paid no attention to the price.

And there was that basket. What did it contain? Amelia thought of petitions, dolls, and dueling pistols, and her knees went as weak as jelly.

Amelia had to confront Millicent. Confront Moreau. She wasn't sure what game either of them was playing, but she struggled to believe that Millicent would hurt her. She sneaked up behind them, and when Pierre went into the shop, Amelia leapt out and caught her friend's arm.

Millicent gasped, and her dragon popped its head out of the basket and hissed in alarm.

"Oh, Amelia!" Millicent didn't look guilty or upset. Her smile glowed as she tucked her dragon back under the cloth. "What are you doing here?"

"What am I… Millicent, dear, do you realize that half the kingdom is looking for you?"

"Looking for me? Really, I cannot believe that Mother and Father would be so vulgar."

"Vulgar? What are you talking about?"

"They must suspect that I eloped, but I cannot imagine them letting the word get around."

"Eloped!" Amelia felt like she'd been knocked back. "Do you mean that you married Pierre Moreau?"

"Of course! Why else would I be with him?"

"Millicent," Amelia struggled to keep her voice low. "Blackerby thinks you are acting as a spy for the Luddites."

Millicent's mouth formed an "o" of shock, and then she laughed. "A spy! What a ridiculous notion. Surely, you didn't believe such a thing."

"No, but it was so strange that you disappeared. And your brother as well."

Millicent made a dismissive motion. "Oh, my brother is probably holed up at the hunting box. Luddites, really! But aren't you going to wish me well?"

"Indeed, I am!" Amelia said sincerely, especially if Moreau was truly innocent. That was what she needed to know. "But what are you doing in Cheapside?"

"We needed a place to hide until we were married, and now that we are, we don't care where we go."

"You didn't have time to elope to Scotland."

"No! We didn't plan anything so melodramatic. Pierre knows a French priest in the neighborhood. It was a Catholic wedding, so an irregular one for an Englishwoman, but Pierre is French, after all. The important thing is that no one can separate us now."

"But what have you been doing all this time?"

Millicent gave her a coy look that made Amelia blush.

Amelia shook her head. "What I mean is, what are you going to do now?"

"We are leaving for the coast tonight. Somewhere close to Lyme Regis, where we first began to realize what we meant to each other. It will be easier to avoid my parents there. Eventually, we must speak to them about some kind of marriage settlement, but I think it best to wait until their ire has cooled. Pierre has rented a little cottage for us with a maid. He is so thoughtful."

Lyme Regis was also an import seaport and a favorite location of smugglers. Could Moreau still be using Millicent? "So, you know nothing about Shaw or the Luddites?"

Millicent frowned. "I have said so. I would hope you, at least, would believe me. You have always been a true friend to me, even when so many others were two-faced."

It struck Amelia that her friend had not yet seen the paper. Didn't know of Amelia's disgrace. "I should tell you some news that will be quite shocking to you."

Millicent raised her eyebrows, looking hungry for gossip, but then realization flickered in her eyes. "Oh, is it that drivel in the papers? Honestly, Amelia, it was in poor taste of you."

"You're... You know it's true and you're not angry with me?"

"For writing silly novels? Why would I be? Besides, I have Pierre now. Nothing else seems to matter."

Amelia stared at Millicent. Perhaps some people really didn't realize that they were being lampooned in the books. Or Millicent was so deeply in love that it painted a glossy lacquer over everything else. It was reassuring to know that Millicent, at least, was not a traitor, and that she harbored no ill will toward Amelia. It was a shame that there was probably no room for Amelia in that cottage of hers.

Pierre Moreau came out from the shop. "I have it all arranged, my love—"

He stopped when he saw Amelia and looked around like he wanted to run. Like he was guilty? But Millicent held her hand out for him, and he took it.

"Dearest Amelia was just congratulating us, love," Millicent said. "Though she seems a trifle distracted with the Luddites."

Moreau waved his hand. "Oh, do not speak to me of Luddites! I thought I had left all of that behind when I fled France. I have no interest in bloodshed, and revolution disrupts one's ability to find a properly tailored suit."

It was a silly sentiment, and yet Amelia detected sincerity in his eyes.

"Indeed," Amelia said. "From whom did you hear of the Luddites?"

Moreau glanced at Millicent, who nodded. "You can tell her whatever you think you ought to."

He looked to Amelia. "It was Monsieur Randolph, you see. He often tried to draw me into conversation about the revolution. Asking if I thought it still would have been so bad if a proper king had been put into place instead of the dictator Napoleon. I told him that the only proper king and queen had been executed. Anyone who replaced them would have been a dictator."

Amelia remembered Moreau and Randolph being at odds with each other. "Could Randolph have imagined himself as a replacement king, do you think?"

Millicent chuckled. "My brother, a king? He has always thought he was better than everyone else. It couldn't happen, though. We're not that closely related to the Prince Regent and dear Princess Charlotte."

"Millicent, dear," Amelia said carefully. "It is possible that your brother is aiding Shaw, trying to overthrow and replace the government."

Something flashed through Millicent's eyes: sadness mingled with anger. She sighed. "I suppose that might be something he would do."

Amelia squeezed her friend's hand. "Can either of you think of something he might have said that could lead us to where Shaw is hiding?"

Millicent shook her head. "I never listened to Randolph."

Moreau looked thoughtful, then his eyes brightened. "Mais oui! He often spoke of meetings held at a tavern near the London Bridge with certain gentlemen interested in knowing more about the revolution in France." He shuddered. "I declined, naturally."

"Do you remember the name of the tavern?" Amelia asked, her heart beating quickly. If Randolph had a meeting place with other revolutionaries, this might be a chance to get ahead of him and Shaw.

But Moreau shook his head. "It has left my mind."

Amelia was disappointed, but she smiled. "Your information could still be very helpful. Thank you! And best of luck to you both."

Millicent embraced her, and she and Moreau vanished down a side alley.

Amelia stood in Fleet Street, staring blankly at the dome of St. Paul's. She was going to have to talk to Blackerby. That meant returning to Mayfair. A few people stared at her as they passed. Her shawl had slipped down, but she pulled it back over her hair.

She would be humiliated if anyone in Mayfair recognized her. But if Blackerby heard that Millicent was in London, he would arrest her. Amelia could tolerate embarrassment—she was used to it—but she could not imagine Millicent arrested. Amelia could intervene, tell Blackerby of the elopement. And if Moreau's information was correct, Amelia might be able to stop Shaw. Wasn't that worth any social price she might have to pay?

She wasn't far from Whitehall. If Blackerby was in his offices, she wouldn't have to return to Mayfair where she was more likely to see people she knew.

With one last glance back at the sanctuary of her cousin's home, she set off for Whitehall. Several men paused to watch her pass. Did they recognize her as the disgraced Lady Amelia? Or as a potential loose woman? Or might they think both were the same? She suddenly felt her vulnerability as a woman walking alone through London. It was one thing when she had been fleeing to a hiding place, but quite another trying to navigate Society totally cut off from everyone.

She decided to hire a boat instead. That would avoid most of the dangers of crowds. She hurried to the waterfront and hailed one of the boats plying the water. The old boatman was more than happy to transport her and didn't even give her a strange look. The things these boatmen must see.

The water seemed choppy, and Amelia clung to the sides of the boat.

"Sorry, miss," the boatman said. "Water's rough today. There's no storm. The tides are acting strangely."

Amelia nodded, but something stirred deep in her, worry worming through her like an eel. What kind of magic might affect the tides? Powerful magic.

Her sense of urgency had built so that by the time they approached Westminster and the ruined hulk of Parliament, she practically tossed the man his money and hurried up the stone steps to the street. She glanced back at the Thames, dark and slippery in the afternoon light. Tightening the shawl over her hair, she almost ran up the street to the Home Office.

She had not counted on the Bow Street Runners. One of their number stood guard in front of the building. No doubt to prevent further Luddite attacks. He gave her a suspicious look. Of course, a well-dressed lady trying to hide her face and wandering alone down the streets would raise any number of questions. Amelia might not seem so different from the woman who had assassinated the Prime Minister. She met the man's eyes and walked directly up to him.

"I need to speak to Lord Blackerby. It's urgent."

"He's not seeing anyone. You can leave a message with me."

That might get her out of having to speak to Blackerby—or anyone else she knew—again. "How soon would he receive the message?"

"Probably tomorrow morning. Maybe tomorrow afternoon if he doesn't come in until then."

Amelia's hope deflated. "But he'll want this information immediately. It's about the Luddites."

The man narrowed his eyes. "Then you can give that information to me, and I'll decide how urgent it is."

"I heard of a place where some of the Luddites may meet."

The man looked more interested at that. "What's the name of this place, then?"

"Well, I don't know the specific name, but I know it's near London Bridge."

The Runner's interest evaporated. "I can pass that on, but His Lordship has more pressing leads to follow at the moment."

"Then can you tell me where he is now?"

"I won't be doing that, miss, but I'll pass on your information to His Lordship when it's convenient."

Amelia growled in her throat, avoiding the desire to stomp her foot. She didn't want to expose Millicent's secrets to this man, and she knew Blackerby would want any hints about the Luddites, even if they didn't seem urgent to the Runner. She was tempted to announce that she was Lord Blackerby's fiancée, but this man wouldn't believe it any more than she did. She would have to find Blackerby herself.

If only she knew how to locate the little street sweep or Brainy Jamie. They always seemed to know where Blackerby was or how to get a message to him. That would be easier than talking to the Westings, too. Street lads didn't care what Amelia wrote.

The last she knew, both boys were at Berkeley Square. Perhaps she could sneak back and find them without encountering anyone else.

Under the suspicious glare of the Bow Street Runner, Amelia turned for Mayfair.

Chapter Seventeen

AMELIA'S FEET ached from trekking all over London. Each step over the uneven stone streets sent tingles of pain up her legs. Urgency pressed on her, propelled her forward like a hand on her back, but her pace was flagging, and it was difficult to move quickly with the many carriages and pedestrians in the street.

She could not take a boat to Mayfair—the river turned the wrong way. A few chairmen stood along the streets with their sedan chairs, but they would not be much faster than her own pace.

An idea came to her. She stepped into a shop and purchased a large straw bonnet—hideously behind the fashion, but it covered her hair and shaded her face decently and looked more respectable than her shawl. She returned to the street to find just the right sort of gentleman.

There! A young whip drove a phaeton with a pair of bays that he struggled to hold back. His fine, but not flashy, suit and cravat imitated the sporting Corinthian set, and he looked likely to drive recklessly. She waved him down.

The young man stopped and looked around as if there might be someone else in his phaeton that she wished to summon. "Do I know you, miss?"

Amelia was very glad for her skills at fiction. "Of course! Do you not remember? We danced at that ball. Oh, which was it?"

The young man looked puzzled for a moment, trying to see her features beneath the bonnet, then his face brightened. "Oh, Cumberland's ball! I do apologize. Didn't mean to cut you."

"No, of course. No offense taken. But I wonder if I might ask you a favor?"

"Anything!" he said earnestly.

"I find myself in an awkward situation. I was separated from my escort, and I need to get quickly to Berkeley Square to see my particular friends, Lord and Lady Westing. Can you take me?"

Excitement lit his face. Westing was a bit of a magical name, especially among the young Corinthians who admired his boxing skills. "Absolutely, Miss, er..."

"Chase. Miss Chase." Better to leave the name Lady Amelia for the newspapers.

He flushed. "So sorry. I'm afraid I might have had too many glasses of wine—" His blush deepened. "Ought not to have said that, miss. So sorry."

"All is forgiven if you can convey me quickly."

"Right!" He motioned for his groom to help Lady Amelia into her seat, and then he set his restless horses into motion.

As Amelia had hoped, he was a reckless driver, quite nearly upsetting the phaeton once, and nearly running down pedestrians on several other occasions. But they reached Berkeley Square in good time, and she directed him to the Westing's townhouse.

"Shall I escort you to the door, miss?" he asked, staring at the house with the sort of awe many reserved for St. James Palace.

He was clearly anxious to glimpse the infamous Westings, but Amelia had no intention of seeing them.

"I've already taken up too much of your time. Thank you so much."

He looked a little disappointed, but he was a gentleman, so he helped her down and tipped his hat to her. She dawdled for a moment as he drove off, then hurried out of sight of the house. She needed one of Blackerby's urchin friends. Or the Runner, Farris. She felt certain they were still watching the house, though all appeared calm there. Had she expected that her departure would turn the whole house inside out? Of course not. They were probably relieved she was gone.

She lurked behind one of the plane trees in the square, feeling rather ridiculous. She was there long enough to see the shadows shift. Long enough for some ladies to pull up in a carriage under the shade of another of the trees and enjoy ices from Gunter's. They laughed and tilted their bonnets closer together to gossip. Were they talking about Miss Charity? Laughing at Lady Amelia?

She pulled back and leaned against the trunk of the tree, its smooth bark mottled with peeling green and brown patches, as though the tree had outgrown its old bark and itched to have it removed. Like a secret wanting to be told. Amelia grabbed the edge of one piece and peeled it away, revealing the smooth, cream-colored bark beneath. Fresh and clean. She cracked the thin sheet of old bark, and it crumbled under her fingers, falling to the ground. She brushed off her hand on her skirt and surveyed the square again.

"Lady Amelia?" Phoebe's gentle voice asked behind her.

Amelia jumped and turned, putting the trunk to her back. Her pulse hammered in her throat. "Lady Westing."

Phoebe sighed. "It's still Phoebe, dear. Are you…do you want to talk?"

Amelia closed her eyes for a moment, taking a deep breath of the earthy, green-scented air of the garden. She didn't want to talk, but she owed it to Phoebe. "I'm sorry. I'm so sorry. I don't know what else I can say."

Phoebe nodded. She placed a hand on her belly and stared absently across the square. "The stories were entertaining. If you hadn't chosen to lampoon so many people…"

Amelia bit her lip. "I enjoyed the writing, but I'm sorry to say I enjoyed making sport of some members of Society as well. Society had no use for me, so I wanted to hold up a mirror… but it wasn't a fair one. Fair to Society, perhaps, but not fair to the individuals in it. I needed a mirror for myself, not for them."

"Oh, Amelia," Phoebe said. "I am sorry. This will go hard on you."

"It is no less than I deserve. Everyone is very vexed at me, I suppose?"

"I was a little hurt, I own, though I can certainly understand why you didn't tell anyone. Eliza is annoyed with you, but..."

"But she never liked me anyway."

Phoebe smiled sadly.

"It is because of Miss Charity that I'm in this whole mess," Amelia said. "I accidentally revealed Randolph Blanchfield as Shaw's co-conspirator, and he's been trying to silence me."

"My goodness!" Phoebe said. "Does Lord Blackerby know?"

Amelia nodded curtly. "And I have discovered more that I need to tell him. I might know a location where we can find something about the Luddites. I need to tell him right away, but I don't know where to find him."

Phoebe bit her lower lip, studying Amelia speculatively. "He stopped by earlier this afternoon. He didn't say it, but I wondered if he was checking on you."

"Oh," Amelia said. Her chest warmed at the idea, but she pushed the feeling aside. "What did you..."

"I told him you had gone out. That you needed time alone." She shrugged one shoulder. "He looked unhappy, but all he said was that he would be at the theater this evening if we needed him."

"At the theater?" Amelia asked. "After the Prime Minister was killed yesterday?"

"He didn't explain why. I doubt he went there for entertainment, though."

"No, you're right, of course. One of the Bow Street Runners told me he was following up on information about the Luddites. But we have to get word to him."

Phoebe nodded. "I'll have Westing call the carriage. Come back inside, dear."

"Lord Westing tried to freeze the door."

"Because I didn't want you to leave like that. I understand now that perhaps a little space was healthy, however. He won't do it again."

Amelia followed Phoebe with great hesitation. She was grateful that Phoebe left her alone in the empty drawing room. Amelia was not

up to any company. It felt like she waited for ages with only the slow
tick of a clock and her own worries for company, but it wasn't more
than half an hour before Phoebe returned in an evening dress to fetch
Amelia. She offered her a hooded cloak to hide her face at the theater.

They met Westing in the entry hall. He gave Amelia a curious look
but said nothing about Miss Charity.

As Westing opened the front door for the ladies, his young brother
Joshua bounded up, a fat tomcat trotting behind him.

"I want to go, too," Joshua said.

"To the theater?" Westing asked skeptically.

"To hunt Shaw and protect the dragons."

"We're not going to hunt anyone," Phoebe said quickly. "Just pass
some information on to Lord Blackerby. It will be very dull."

Joshua pouted and scooped up Tom to pet him with his good hand
as he watched the party descend the stairs.

Westing helped Phoebe and Amelia into his phaeton. It was only
meant for two, but it would be more maneuverable than a larger coach
for making their way through the crowded streets. When Westing
climbed in and took the reins, the party was quite pinched together.
Amelia, on the end, felt like she was dangling half-out of the phaeton.

Phoebe giggled.

"What are you laughing at, wife?" Westing asked, his tone sharp,
but his lips curled up at the corners.

"I am remembering the first time I saw you, and you raced past
Max's gig when we had Deborah stuffed in it beside me, and you
probably thought we looked ridiculous, three people crammed into
such a small vehicle."

"Nonsense!" he said with a sly smile. "You appeared so low and
dismal, I didn't think of you at all."

Phoebe laughed. "Oh, no! I saw the look you gave us. You were
thinking any number of haughty things about us."

"I am glad to have been utterly wrong."

They smiled at each other. Amelia suppressed a sigh. She had no
one to laugh with, and soon she would be sent away where she never
would. She had been able to make Lord Blackerby laugh, but she
would be useless to him after tonight. She doubted he would even

want to see her in public with the Miss Charity scandal hot on everyone's lips. But if he wouldn't listen to her, at least he might have to listen to Westing.

They arrived at Brydges-street, where the Theatre Royal blazed with candlelight in the dusk and members of the *haut ton* came and went from the blocky front entrance. Amelia pulled up her borrowed hood, hoping to stay anonymous. Thankfully, Lord Blackerby's theater box would be easy enough to find.

Westing escorted Phoebe and Amelia through the grand entrance hall and up the stairs to the boxes. It was between acts, and the hall was crowded with people leaving early or making their way to the rotunda. People who would recognize Lady Amelia. She kept her head down and followed Phoebe and Westing to Blackerby's box.

Westing peered inside, and Amelia stood on tiptoe to see over his shoulder. The candles were out, the box still and empty.

"Confound the man!" Westing said.

Phoebe put a soothing hand on his arm. "We just have to find him. Look, there's Aunt Seraphina and Uncle Jasper. Perhaps they've seen him."

Amelia hung back. Lord and Lady Jasper had appeared in Miss Charity's novels as well, and she thought it wise not to let them see her. She stepped into Blackerby's box. The scent of Blackerby's eau de cologne mingled with the smoke from the many candles. He had been there recently. Keeping her hood low, Amelia scanned the bright theater. She spotted a familiar figure in a box opposite. Blackerby. He was not looking her way, talking to someone else. A woman.

Amelia's stomach twisted, and she turned away. He had snuffed the candles in his own box. Did that mean he was not coming back to it? They had to catch him.

Amelia hurried out of the box, looking for any sign of Phoebe and Westing. Where had they gone?

She hitched up her hood and scurried down the corridor, dodging theatergoers. Farther down, she spotted Blackerby's graceful form in a swooping black cloak. But he was walking away from his box, like he was leaving. That would not do. Amelia called after him, but she was afraid to raise her voice much and call attention to herself. He did not turn. She muttered some unladylike words under her breath and hurried after him.

He turned down a side passage, and Amelia hesitated. This path seemed to go into the bowels of the theater. Did Blackerby have a female friend among the actresses? It would be a good source of information, yet the thought made Amelia's stomach seethe. She stormed after him.

Her footsteps echoed in the corridor, cut off as it was from the crowds and not so nicely carpeted or well lit. A figure loomed in front of her.

"Lord Blackerby!" she gasped in surprise.

A hand caught her wrist.

"You guessed incorrectly," hissed a smooth voice out of the darkness.

The figure that had seemed so like Blackerby's suddenly changed into someone shorter, less lithe.

"Who are you?" Amelia said.

"Just a former actor. I always did have a knack for impersonations. I can't mimic the earl's shadows, but moving quickly in a crowd, you don't have time to notice that detail."

He was right. Amelia cursed her foolishness. This man had shown her what she hoped to see. "You are Shaw."

"I have been known by that name. And you are Miss Charity."

"I tend *not* to be known by that name."

"Yes, we know about moving in the shadows, don't we?"

"You've been hunting me."

"Not at all. I don't really care about you one way or the other. Randolph Blanchfield is the one obsessed with silencing you. But you have become involved, and I can't have that."

He was going to kill her. Amelia saw it clearly, but she felt oddly calm about it. Maybe she had become used to people trying to kill her. She only thought that she had rather not die in the back corridors of a theater. It was not a proper place for a girl of her standing to be killed. How the newspapers would love the story: the disgraced Miss Charity murdered in a shocking scandal. She did not want to give them the satisfaction.

She yanked her hand free and raced down the corridor, only to collide with a tall figure.

"Blackerby!" she said.

"No, Amelia," Randolph's voice said from the darkness.

She backed away so she could see his face. His cold eyes glittered in the faint light from the end of the corridor. She opened her mouth to scream for help, even knowing that no one was likely to hear her, but Randolph slapped her, making spots flash in front of her eyes.

"You have caused me a great deal of trouble, Amelia. Not very kind of you." He stepped closer. "I can't have you spreading more tales."

She laughed weakly. "The irony is that I didn't even know you were a traitor." Her voice sounded serene to her ears, as though they were simply in a drawing-room, and Shaw wasn't creeping up behind her. Both exits were now blocked. "I only had you acting the part because you were so unkind to Millicent."

"I'll be glad enough to be rid of you anyway. You always were looking down your nose at me. I don't know a young man who would stand for your condescension."

"And I always thought it was the red hair."

Shaw was right behind her now. Randolph reached for something. A pistol, perhaps.

Amelia grabbed the fan from her chatelaine and jabbed it into Randolph's throat. He choked and doubled forward, clutching his throat. Amelia lunged around him. Something jerked her head back, wrenching her neck and bringing tears to her eyes. Someone had her by the hair. Shaw.

Shaw hauled her back. "Have you killed Blanchfield, I wonder?"

He continued to hold her scalp captive while he examined Randolph writhing on the ground. "No. You hurt him but failed to collapse his windpipe." Shaw shook his head. "You shouldn't have thought of using a pistol in here, Blanchfield," he said in an off-handed way. "Much too loud. We will dispose of Lady Amelia elsewhere. She might even make a good piece of bait or bargaining chip. You've always been too hasty."

Randolph glared daggers at Amelia as he struggled to his feet, and she instinctively shrank nearer to Shaw, who at least wasn't going to kill her immediately. She could call for help as soon as they were out of the corridor.

But Shaw wrapped a gag around her mouth and roughly twisted her arms behind her to bind them together. A distant part of her mind thought that these details would be excellent in one of her books, but a voice nearer to rationality reminded her that she had written her last.

She kicked wildly at both men, but Shaw—surprisingly strong—lifted her over his shoulder, and all she could do was squirm helplessly and try to chew through the thick, dirty-tasting rag in her mouth. Shaw dragged her deeper into the dark corridor.

Chapter Eighteen

BLACKERBY ALWAYS TRIED to be on guard, but nothing prepared him for being accosted by Deborah Shaw in the rotunda of the Theatre Royal.

"Lord Blackerby!" Miss Shaw threw herself in his path, with Max Hart panting behind her as he caught up. She turned big, blue eyes filled with tears to him. "Please tell me Lady Amelia has found you."

Blackerby's chest tightened at the thought of Lady Amelia at the theater. After the Miss Charity debacle, it would be like tossing a wounded dove to a clowder of cats. "Was Lady Amelia seeking me?"

"She came to find you," Max said, holding his side and gasping to catch his breath.

Blackerby felt an odd constriction in his throat. "Why would she risk that?"

"It's my uncle," Miss Shaw wailed. "She thinks she discovered where he is. She told Lady Westing, and they set out to find you."

"And Phoebs and West didn't bring us along, can you imagine?" Max asked.

"Er, but you came anyway," Blackerby said.

"I must help stop my uncle!" Deborah said. "I'm certain it's my destiny to right the wrongs of my family."

"We ran here," Max said.

"I… see," Blackerby said. "Yet I have not seen the Westings, either."

"Something has gone wrong," Deborah said to Max.

Blackerby sighed. "Stand back."

He closed his eyes and let the theater's shadows flow toward him. He was distantly aware of gasps and people shuffling back from him, but he was used to it by now, even took a perverse pleasure in their discomfort. He couldn't make people like him, but at least they could respect him.

The shadows were eager, hungry tonight. People sometimes made the mistake of thinking that the darkness wanted to stay hidden, but secrets long to be told, lies strained to be revealed. And Blackerby could hear them. The problem was to keep himself from going mad with the things that they whispered. He had to tease out just what he needed and not let the darkness control him.

He ran the images through his mind like fingers through falling sand, trying to pick out the grain he needed. He sensed light very close. Phoebe Westing. His display had brought her, and likely Westing, too. They were not lost, then. But what of Lady Amelia? The darkness liked her. Liked her secrets. He sensed Shade bolt away from him, and he opened his eyes.

The shadows settled in the clear space around him. A crowd gawked. This was as good as the evening's entertainment for them. He scanned the faces until he spotted Westing and his wife.

"Where is Lady Amelia?" he asked.

Phoebe shook her head, her eyes full of concern. "She came with us, but we can't find her now. Since she was looking for you…"

"One would expect her to see the shadows and find me," Blackerby said, cold worry climbing his spine. "Which way did my dragon go?"

Westing pointed toward the back of the theater. Blackerby jogged after Shade, his long legs covered the ground quickly. He found Shade pacing in front of a closed door. Blackerby drew his pistol and pushed the door open.

The corridor was empty.

But not long ago, it had not been. The shadows danced, performing a pantomime for him of recent events. Ghostly shadow figures showed a woman trying to escape, only to be cut off by two male figures.

Possibly Lady Amelia, though he wasn't sure why she would be lurking in the back corridors of the theater. It could be some other woman.

Blackerby.

The echo of Lady Amelia's voice reached him.

And I always thought it was the red hair.

A different voice: *Have you killed Blanchfield I wonder.*

He couldn't piece together the whole conversation, but he recognized the traces of Shaw, sensed the strange absence of emotion that he left behind.

Blackerby took off at a run down the corridor. Voices—real voices—called behind him, but he only motioned them to follow. He burst out of the back of the theater and stood in an alley, scanning the shadows. No echoes of a carriage.

"Blackerby?" Westing's voice came from behind him.

"I believe Shaw has her, fleeing on foot. They could not have gone far. But which direction?"

The shadows here were too mixed up and crisscrossed for their trail to be clear. Shade paced the ground and hissed in frustration.

A light grew above them, courtesy of Lady Westing. Her face was grim in the brightness. Deborah looked determined, Max angry. But their emotions lacked direction.

"My lady!" A lad bounded up to them. Brainy Jamie with another ragged street boy.

"Jamie!" Phoebe stepped forward. "Why are you here?"

"He made me do it." The urchin pointed to the scruffy boy next to him, who looked up at them with equal parts defiance and fear, a missing hand and a familiar face under the dirty disguise.

"Joshua!" Westing roared. "What on earth—"

"I knew you would need help," Joshua said. "And I knew Jamie could get us here and see things that you would miss."

"Well, and did you?" Blackerby said before Westing could scold his young half-brother.

"We saw them!" Jamie said. "They went toward the river. I 'ad a friend try to follow 'em, but they gave 'im the slip."

"Are they escaping by boat?" Phoebe asked. "Maybe for France?"

"Why would they need Lady Amelia in France?" Max asked.

"They won't," Deborah wailed. "They'll kill her and dump her in the river."

For once, Blackerby was seized with a desire to shake the girl into silence. But only because he feared she was right.

He whirled on Joshua and Brainy Jamie. "Go, find the Bow Street Runner Farris and tell him what has happened. Tell him I want everyone on the streets looking for them."

The boys nodded, their eyes bright with excitement, and they dashed off.

He raced toward the river, past Somerset House overlooking the water, and to the banks of the Thames. Boats plied their trade up and down the river. It was impossible to know if Shaw or Lady Amelia was on any of them. At least he didn't see any signs of a disturbance, which a murder on the riverbank surely must have caused.

Frantic voices called from the river. Blackerby swore. Was Shaw out there hurting Lady Amelia now? Wishing for the power to fly, he ran toward Somerset House where the Navy had its headquarters, determined to steal a boat if he had to.

More shouts came across the water. They sounded more panicked than Blackerby would expect from violence on the water. Like they were warning of a threat. Westing's party caught up with Blackerby. They stood in silence, scanning the waters that rolled through the city like sluggish, black blood.

A purple dragon soared overhead and came to rest on Lady Westing's shoulder.

"It's Eliza's dragon!" Lady Westing said, studying the creature in surprise.

"It has something in its mouth," Westing said.

He reached out, but the dragon shied from him. Lady Westing held her hand out, and the dragon dropped a rather crumpled piece of paper into it. She ignited a glowing sphere overhead and read the letter. Her eyes widened, and she looked up at the group.

"Eliza says to stay away from the water. She says there's some great danger or upset stirring."

"Shaw," Blackerby said.

Joshua yelped and pointed across the inky blackness. Something roiled in the water. Boatmen screamed as their barges lurched upward, some rolling onto their side to dump people into the waters. A great two-masted ship capsized slowly, its sails turning over into the water like the blades of a mill. Sailors and passengers shouted for help.

"There's something in there!" someone shouted.

But they didn't need the warning. They could see the smooth scales, slippery and damp under the faint moonlight and the light from the boats. It glided smoothly, like a great water serpent the length of a palace.

Then a tail flicked up out of the water and capsized a slew of boats.

Miss Shaw shrieked, and Blackerby went cold at the sight. A great water beast making its way up the Thames, ready to attack London. And he had no doubt who was behind it.

Chapter Nineteen

BLACKERBY WRENCHED his gaze away from the churning chaos of the Thames. Shaw was... where? He didn't have to be close to be in contact with the dragon, Blackerby guessed, but he also couldn't have gone far if he had just abducted Lady Amelia. And, based on the echoes Blackerby had heard from the shadows, Randolph Blanchfield was with him.

Blackerby sent his shadows off to sweep the local area, but all they relayed back to him were the general shudders of chaos rocking the riverbanks, spreading like tremors through the city as people came out to investigate the yelling. Shaw wanted chaos, and he had brought it into the heart of London, the heart of England.

The ground rumbled beneath them, sending ripples over the water like the wrinkles in a lady's silk dress. Blackerby paced the bank, his only thought to reach Amelia. To reach Shaw. It was all the same. He had to save her and England both.

Another rumble sent him stumbling off balance, and lightning flashed across the sky.

"What's happening?" Westing called over the noise of dogs barking madly and birds waking from their roosts and cawing.

"It's the end of the world!" Deborah wailed.

Blackerby spun, restraining his desire to shake the girl. "It is not! Tell me what any of you knew of Lady Amelia's information. Surely, she told you something?"

Phoebe looked thoughtful. "She mentioned London Bridge. I should have pressed her for more details, but I didn't think."

"Never mind. We head toward Southwark." There were plenty of places around the docks for Shaw to hide, but if they were closer, Blackerby might sense something more from the shadows. He might find Lady Amelia before it was too late.

Blackerby wanted to take the river, which would be faster, but people fled the waters, scrambling for the safety of land. He led the little band along the roads running close to the Thames.

"Wait!" a female voice called.

Blackerby turned to see Eliza and Captain Parry running up to them.

"Where are you going?" Captain Parry called.

"Southwark," Blackerby responded. "It would be faster if we could go by water."

Eliza looked skeptical. "I can try to guide our passage, but I can't promise our safety."

Blackerby scowled at the streets crowded with pedestrians and carriages. "Time is of the essence. A trip up the river sounds delightful."

Eliza nodded, and they all went down to the bank. It was not hard to find an abandoned boat, and they quickly climbed in.

"Grab oars," Captain Parry ordered, in his element, and the men obeyed, Westing, Max Hart, and Blackerby joining him to steer the barge into the waters.

The tide was in their favor, and it moved them swiftly along, thanks no doubt to Eliza's magic. She was staring very hard at the murky black waters, her hands moving gently as if trying to swim through the air. They shot under the arches of Black Friars Bridge with more skill than they had any right to.

Then, Eliza's face went pale, and she stumbled. Her husband dropped his oar to catch her before she fainted.

"Liza!" Parry called as the others paddled in circles.

Eliza's eyes fluttered open. "We have to stop," she said hoarsely. "It's up ahead, in the water."

Blackerby looked ahead at the churning water near the construction debris where the new Southwark Bridge was being built. A long, serpentine tail lashed out of the water, splashing down to send waves pounding against their little barge.

"Paddle to shore!" Parry called.

Westing and Blackerby put their backs into it, and the shore drew closer. The creature in the water circled, creating a whirlpool that dragged at them. Despite their best efforts, they drew no closer to the shore, perhaps even inched farther from it.

Westing tossed down his oar and held his hands out. The air turned icy cold, and a bridge of ice crackled out over the surface of the water, connecting the barge to the land. When Blackerby hesitated at the slick surface, spikes of ice rose from the bridge, enough to help a person keep his balance.

"Go!" Westing shouted.

Blackerby went first to test its strength, and when the ice held him, he motioned for the women to follow. Eliza and Westing came last, combining the efforts of their magic to keep them from being swept up by the monster in the water.

Blackerby was grateful to reach dry earth again, but the ground trembled beneath him again, more violently than before. An answering crack of thunder split the night. Shade turned his head skyward and made an odd, chirping noise, flapping his wings restlessly.

The other dragons did the same. Then, they took flight as if pulled by a single mind. Blackerby had a brief fear that Shaw had learned to control the wills of dragons. But they did not head for the water. Instead, they flew east. Toward the Tower of London.

In the moonlight, he caught glimpses of other dragons circling the Tower like graceful birds of prey.

Tingles ran down Blackerby's spine. The Tower Dragon. The great White Dragon of England. It was said to communicate with other dragons. It was said to be ready to defend England in her most dire hour.

It was also buried deep under the White Tower. Was it rallying all the young dragons of the kingdom to fight, then?

He wanted to leave the fight to the dragons and hunt for Shaw and Lady Amelia. Duty be hanged. But he needed information, and the Tower was where he was likely to find it.

"Follow them!" Blackerby shouted, and he ran through the alleys behind warehouses and along Lower Thames Street to the gates of the Tower.

It was fully dark, and the Beefeaters guarding the Tower would be locking everything up.

He rattled the closed gate. "Open up! In the name of the King!"

A guard came puffing down the narrow, stone street of the tower complex. "Who's there, then?"

"The Earl of Blackerby, Secretary of the Home Office in the service of His Majesty, King George. Open these gates."

The man looked shaken, and he fumbled with the brass keys in his hands. "How do I know you're really Lord Blackerby?"

Blackerby rolled his eyes. Shadows swarmed the guard like a plague of locusts.

The man yelped and swatted at them. "Right away, my lord. Opening the gate. It's been a strange enough night." He stopped and stared behind Blackerby at the bridge over the moat. "What about them, then?"

Blackerby turned to look past his party and saw several well-dressed gentlemen and ladies converging on the Tower. Most watched the dragons circling overhead. One lady held out a hand for a dragon that landed on her outstretched arm. He recognized Mrs. Reynolds.

"Anyone with a dragon gets inside," Blackerby said.

The guard looked like he wanted to argue, but then he glanced at the dragons circling overhead and shrugged. "As long as it's on your orders, my lord."

Blackerby didn't understand what was happening either, but if the Great Dragon was calling all the dragon-linked there, then the Great Dragon would have them. An army of magic-wielding men and women and their dragons.

Blackerby strode through the interior gates of the tower, across the rough stone streets, and up the hill to the threshold of the White Tower to look out over the dark waters. Shade circled down and landed on his shoulder. The other dragons rejoined their masters once they reached the Tower walls. Shade made his odd chirping noise again, and the Tower ravens fluttered and cawed restlessly. Blackerby didn't consider himself superstitious, but if the ravens left, the Tower was supposed to fall. And if the Tower fell, so would England.

Don't leave. Blackerby found himself urging them.

The ground trembled. He braced himself. Was this Shaw's doing? Or, was the White Dragon stirring? He peered down between the White Tower and the Thames where the great dragon was thought to rest. It was believed to be attuned to earth, though no one knew for certain. The beast had slept for so long, all that was left were rumors. But if it was an earth dragon, their experience with Eliza Parry meant that the Prince Regent should be able to communicate with the dragon since they shared an attunement. The idiot was probably too drunk to notice that his dragon was gone. If it was even able to fly anymore. Blackerby would have to send someone to fetch him.

The earth rumbled again. Deborah shouted, her hysterical screams rising into the night.

"It *is* the end of the world!" she cried.

Blackerby raced over, his long strides quickly bringing him to where the other dragon-linked—two-dozen or so people—were gathered on the far side of the White Tower.

A huge crack ran the length of the ground, splitting cobblestones as if they were wafers. They gaped apart like sharp, crooked teeth.

"What's happening?" Westing shouted to Blackerby over the grinding of the earth.

"I believe we misunderstood where the White Dragon was sleeping."

Lightning split the sky, making the scene as bright as day for a moment. Blackerby caught just a glimpse of the ground below, a deep chasm, the dirt falling away as if into hell itself.

Deborah gaped. "I can hear it!" She looked at the others. "Can't you hear it?"

Blackerby stared at her. "I cannot," he said slowly. "What is it saying?"

"It is asking what has awakened it. It says... it says it senses chaos has approached its shores. Oh, pardon me. *It* is a *he*."

Everyone stared at her, and she flushed. "I don't understand why you can't hear it, too. It is quite clear. Its voice seems to take up my whole head, in fact."

Eliza Parry stepped forward, her purple dragon on her arm like a falcon. "That was how it was when I communicated with the water dragon."

Blackerby sighed. "Legend has served us a poor turn. Our great dragon is not an earth dragon. It is a storm dragon. And Miss Shaw, you are the only one here attuned to storms."

Her eyes widened. "Lightning. I'm attuned to lightning."

"A manifestation of the sky and storms. Quickly, you must explain to it—in your mind—what is happening."

She nodded and wrinkled her brow as if trying to push her thoughts out into the world. Blackerby grinned at the notion that the ancient and venerable creature below them was receiving an earful of Deborah's dramatics. Hopefully, it had a sense of humor.

"It says to stand back," Deborah said, looking around at everyone. "Well back."

The gathered crowd seemed to guess what that meant, and they scurried as far from the gap in the ground as they could manage. Blackerby backed up and braced himself against the wall of the White Tower.

The crack shuddered, and then stones and dirt rolled out like a wave of lava from deep within the earth. The creature's claw appeared first. Blackerby's heartbeat stuttered at the size of that claw, the talons as long as he was. Yes, dragons continued to grow as they slept beneath the earth. The talons dug into the ground, and the earth heaved upwards as it birthed the enormous head of the creature, followed by a long, thick body, and a tail that seemed to go on and on.

Free of its resting place, the dragon shook itself, scattering a shower of dirt and pebbles over the ruptured courtyard. The sound of them pattering to the ground was the only thing that broke the deep silence hanging over the crowd of dragon-linked. The dragon stretched out its wings, and they shadowed the courtyard like a lunar eclipse.

Yet the dragon itself seemed to glow. It was silver. Pure silver. Blackerby had long speculated that white was the dragon's juvenile color and not a reflection of its mature hue—white would indicate it was attuned to ice—but he had never imagined the perfect, shimmering silver of an ancient storm dragon. It lowered its wings, again letting the moon shine in the courtyard, and its scales glittered in the light.

The dragon roared, and thunder answered its call.

"What now?" Westing asked once the echoes died down.

The shadows danced around Blackerby, and he smiled, "My dears, now is the time to use our gifts in the service of our country. I believe we have been summoned to war."

Chapter Twenty

THE GREAT DRAGON of England was not a flier. Blackerby was a little disappointed, but he imaged the creature's wings were weak after sleeping for so long. The mighty beast lumbered across the courtyard of the Tower of London and raised its huge, silvery body up to perch like a monstrous cat on the Byward Tower above the moat and the main entrance to the complex.

And then it opened its jaws and breathed lightning into the air.

The air crackled and split, sending waves of dry friction over Blackerby's skin.

A roar and splash from the river answered. The chaos dragon.

The dragon-linked ran to the south battlements, climbing medieval stairs to the crenelated stone walls overlooking the dark waters. Blackerby took a position near the Salt Tower, at the end of the south wall farthest from the dragon so he could oversee the action. The Thames churned against the wharf, lapping angrily around the Traitor's Gate below. Moonlight glinted off its surface.

Shaw had to be nearby. Blackerby listened to the shadows for some clue about Lady Amelia's whereabouts, but they only snickered and mocked him.

The light took on a reddish cast. A gasp rustled through the gathered dragon-linked, and Blackerby looked up. Red swirled across the moon's face like a wheel of flames. Blackerby drew a sharp breath. He had never seen anything like it.

"It *is* the end of the world," Deborah Shaw said from somewhere nearby. She glanced defensively at Blackerby. "It's not just me saying that—the White Dragon fears it."

Blackerby heard echoes of laughter from the shadows.

"No!" he called down the line. "The red mist is a trick of the chaos dragon."

Phoebe Westing created a burning light overhead. More red mists swirled around the yellow orb, threatening to obliterate it. Lady Westing cried out in alarm.

But another light arose to merge with hers and strengthen it.

Blackerby scanned the figures on the walls, and spotted Lady Millicent there. His first instinct was to question her, but they could not afford the distraction at the moment, and she appeared to be aiding them. Millicent met Phoebe's gaze, and the two rivals nodded at each other.

The combined light glowed brighter, bursting through the tangle of red mists and providing enough illumination for everyone to see the creature below them. Its long, snake-like body wrapped around the London Bridge, a multitude of shimmering colors reflecting off its wet scales. It roared again, and Blackerby would have sworn he heard mad, gibbering voices in the sound. Where the chaos dragon touched the old structure, the rocks slowly crumbled, splashing into the water below.

The creature's tail skirted along several warehouses on the docks, and the buildings crumpled as though burned.

Blackerby's chest tightened. It was as if the creature's touch could dissolve the world into its base elements.

The White Dragon bellowed and breathed lightning at the chaos dragon. The flash split the darkness, and the chaos dragon shrieked in pain. The sky rumbled, the clouds churning with red.

The chaos dragon lifted its head and roared, an answering blast of lightning crackling across the water and exploding against the wharf below.

Blackerby cursed to himself. The creature could use lightning as well. It would lay all of London to waste.

Eliza Parry leaned forward and gestured, and a huge wave rolled along the Thames to slam the chaos dragon loose from the London Bridge.

It lurched into the water with a splash that sent waves careening in every direction. Then it rolled and brought its serpentine head up to fix its black eyes on the Tower. Blackerby nodded. Yes, keep it focused on them and not on the city.

Tentacles extended from the beast's body like snakes reaching over the water. It opened its mouth and blasted a spray of hot water against the tower. Steam filled the air, along with the stench of decay so strong that Blackerby choked on it and brought his sleeve to his nose.

Shouts bounced off the walls of the Tower as various of the dragon-linked pointed this way or that. Blackerby couldn't see what alarmed them, only more red mist rolling along the banks of the river, but his sense of chittering voices in the shadows strengthened.

"That can't be," Captain Parry's voice came to him from nearby.

"What do you see?" Blackerby asked.

The captain glanced in his direction, then fixed his good eye back on the water below. "Men lost at sea long ago. Men I knew. The sea is giving up its dead!"

"I see my father and brother, too," Lord Westing said, his voice tight.

Blackerby still saw nothing but red mist. But he knew no one lost at sea. The shadows laughed and cavorted along the edges of the wharf.

The voices in the dark grew stronger.

Lord of Darkness. Come to us. Join us.

If he let the darkness in, it would make him wiser. Stronger. Was there anything more powerful than darkness?

Light.

The word came to him as though whispered in his ear. He imagined Lady Amelia's voice, her breath warm against his cheek. If he let the darkness in, he didn't know that he would ever rid himself of it, and then how could he be worthy of her?

Blackerby shook his head to clear his thoughts and looked back at the ranks of the dragon-linked mired in fear and confusion.

"It's another illusion!' he called, though he didn't know for certain it was true. "We must contain the chaos dragon. Do not let it touch the land."

Westing's face hardened, and he gestured, sending a wave of ice over the water to smash into the chaos dragon. The water around the beast grew solid, and it struggled to free itself. It roared, and lightning from its jaws cracked the darkness.

The White Dragon roared back, striking the water with a blast of lightning. The ice around the chaos dragon exploded, but the red mists evaporated.

"They're gone!" Captain Parry said.

The chaos dragon turned to face the White Dragon. The White Dragon spread its wings wide, as if daring the chaos dragon to attack. The beast in the water lashed its tentacles forward to grip the Byward Tower. The stones of the tower began to crumble. The White Dragon swiped its talons, cutting one tentacle loose, and then another.

The chaos dragon parted its jaws and hissed a blast of bitter cold. It knocked the White Dragon back, encasing half of its body in ice. The White Dragon fell from its perch on the tower.

Deborah Shaw screamed in pain. Her eyes rolled back in her head, and she collapsed into Max Hart's arms.

Shards of ice exploded against the stone walls. Blackerby ducked behind a crenelation, and a spear of ice shattered beside him. Several of the dragon-linked cried out in pain.

Lightning, water, ice. Could the chaos dragon command all the elements? All of the ones the dragon-linked had mastered.

Blackerby's stomach turned as he understood, and he jumped to his feet, scanning the walls for Mrs. Reynolds. She was running toward the chaos dragon, a ball of fire burning above her hand, ready to strike.

"Mrs. Reynolds, stop!" Blackerby shouted, forcing the wild shadows ahead to circle her.

Her steps faltered, and she looked back.

"It can use whatever we hit it with," Blackerby called. "Don't give it any more elements. Especially not fire. Use water and ice to contain it."

"But how do we stop it?" Westing called.

Blackerby glanced at the White Dragon struggling to snap free from the rest of the ice trapping its wing. It was an ancient creature, unable to stop the chaos dragon on its own. The Byward Tower rumbled ominously beside it, several chunks of stone crashing to the ground.

That was the way of chaos. It was like darkness. It was always inching forward, always hungry, always consuming. You didn't vanquish it; you merely held it at bay. Westing and all these others, whose gifts were about giving order to the elements, they would not understand that. Blackerby understood it, because he understood the darkness.

"You don't stop it," Blackerby called. "You merely delay it. Keep it distracted from harming the city. I have to find Shaw to end this."

And, heavens willing, he would find Lady Amelia as well.

Chapter Twenty-One

AMELIA SAT BOUND in a warehouse near the docks, trying to wiggle her hands free and desperate to find out what was happening outside. The warehouse was one large room transformed into a labyrinth by stacks of barrels and crates. Its few windows were too small and high for Amelia to see anything except an occasional flash of lightning, though Shaw and Randolph watched out one window through a spyglass. At least they weren't paying much attention to her. Her hands were bound behind her, and they had wrapped ropes around her waist and tied her down on a hard, cold seat with no back. If she could get her hands free, she thought she could undo the other ropes, too.

The ropes scraped her wrists into blistering pain, and her shoulders throbbed from straining against her bonds. She gave them a break and returned to chewing at the soggy cloth pressed into her mouth. Her tongue felt raw, and her jaw ached from the grinding, but she had worked her way through some of the fibers. She might get the thing out before they killed her.

The ground rumbled beneath them again. A dark red mist hung over everything. Amelia wanted to scream at the frustration of not knowing what was happening. Were her friends fighting Shaw's dragon? Was Blackerby? They would need to find Shaw. If only she could help. She grunted in frustration against the gag.

The river's heavy odor of fish and sewer filled her nose, but otherwise, her only clues about anything came from Randolph's occasional commentary, and she struggled to believe half the things he said.

He chuckled. "Our dragon has dealt a fine blow to the White Dragon. It won't be long now before they're defeated."

No, he had to be lying. The White Dragon wouldn't fall. And if there were dragon-linked out there fighting, as Amelia guessed, they would never step aside for Shaw. Not the Westings or the Parrys. Not Blackerby.

Shaw stood watching the window and listening to Randolph's reports. He said nothing, but his clenched fists often twitched, though in frustration or triumph, Amelia couldn't guess. His face revealed nothing.

If they truly had unleashed a chaos dragon on London, they must have used the Stone of Scone. But where could it be? She couldn't see it in the warehouse, though it could be anywhere. But neither of them was touching anything so obvious.

She gave her teeth a rest and went back to wiggling her hands. The rope cut into her skin, raw and stinging, but she kept up the small, painful movements. She had managed to make her bonds a little looser, and she didn't need Shaw or Randolph to realize it. If she was lucky, they would forget her entirely.

The air crackled and thunder boomed overhead, rattling the windows of the building.

"The White Dragon isn't giving up yet." Randolph's head whipped around, and he eyed Shaw. "If that dragon doesn't surrender to us, it will doom all of our plans. The Prince Regent will never relinquish the throne if the dragon fights for him."

Shaw waved his hand dismissively. "That dragon is old, weak from its years sleeping. The chaos dragon can easily defeat it."

"Our dragon is also old, from what you've told me, and has been sleeping almost as long."

Shaw's teeth flashed in the dimness. "But chaos never weakens. It is the most enduring and powerful of all the elements. Chaos was here when the universe began, and it will outlast us all. Our chaos dragon will kill the White Dragon—absorb and destroy its element and its magic as it destroys everything else."

Randolph shifted. "I do not want to rule over a kingdom of chaos. If the White Dragon falls—"

"We will start a new kingdom."

"One built on chaos?"

"A new order to emerge from the chaos."

"That is not what we agreed." Randolph's eyes narrowed. "But it's what you planned all along. Where do I fit in this new order of yours?"

"A peer among equals. A place on the council."

Randolph's face reddened. Amelia felt a stab of sympathy for him. He had been used, and now he knew it. "You could not have awakened the chaos dragon without my bloodline. You need me, and you will listen to me—"

Shaw drew a pistol and shot Randolph in the chest.

Randolph staggered back, his mouth moving in silent shock as he pressed his hands to his heart. Blood seeped between his fingers. Amelia stifled a gasp. She had not been fond of who Randolph became —even before she knew he was a traitor and a murderer—but she saw now in his fear and confusion the boy he had once been, and she wished she could reach out and comfort that lost child.

Randolph turned to face her, as if he wanted to share the shock and dismay of the moment with someone. He took several uneven steps and sank to the ground near her feet.

"I have grown weary of you, my lord," Shaw said coolly. "And I no longer need you. My new kingdom does not have a place for you after all."

He walked past Randolph's dying form and stood before Amelia. Her eyes fixed on the pistol in his hand. Shaw had no use for her, either. This was it then. Her writing—her words—had brought this trouble on her, after a lifetime of feeling like no one was listening, but she didn't want to die silent.

She chewed at the gag, tearing bits of fabric loose and swallowing them, trying not to choke on the sodden clumps of cloth in her throat.

The threads pressed against her tongue. So thin, fragile. She ground her teeth down on them, snapping them one by one until the gag fell loose. She spit it out.

"Only a coward would kill a helpless woman," she snapped at Shaw.

He cocked his head. "I'm not going to kill you yet. At the moment, you're useful to me."

"I have no intention of helping you," Amelia said, forcing her eyes away from Randolph. "Whatever you said to convince Randolph, it won't work on me."

He chuckled coldly. "I don't have to convince you. You're sitting on the Stone of Destiny at this very moment, your noble blood stirring the chaos dragon."

Amelia gasped and rocked to the side, trying to look at her hard seat. Hard as a stone. She might have guessed, though she had not imagined Shaw leaving her so close to his stolen treasure. She was bound to the iron ring-handles on either side of it, apparently lending animation to the chaos dragon whether she wanted to or not.

"I won't command it to hurt anyone," she said.

"No, I expect you wouldn't. Though why you care is beyond me. Society has not been kind to you. A new kingdom would benefit you more than any claim to noble blood ever has. But I don't need you to command the dragon. I only need it awake. It will do enough destruction without any extra urging. You may sit on this makeshift throne and enjoy knowing that London is paying for its sins."

Amelia felt icy at his words, but she pushed her own fears aside to focus on Shaw. She had misjudged so often, she did not trust her instincts now. But Shaw, for all his coolness, harbored a core of anger—a cold fire that had burned away everything else.

"Your family lost their lawsuit," she said. "The one that your father brought before Parliament."

Shaw's eyes narrowed, then he smirked. "Your precious Blackerby has done some digging, I take it. My father was foolish to even try to bring a suit against a dragon-linked peer. Of course he lost. And Parliament didn't care when we lost everything in a mysterious flood while our water-attuned lord-neighbor's lands were untouched."

"So, you're seeking revenge."

"Revenge is futile. I'm seeking justice. My father shot himself after we lost our home. I have done everything since then to keep my family alive. Working in the theater. Spying for anyone willing to pay. Learning the ways of Society. And now, I ensure my family's future by removing the dragon-linked from the equation."

Shaw walked back to the window on the other side of the room, leaving Amelia secured on the Stone of Scone. She glared after him, but he didn't care. He knew she was trapped. She tried rocking herself off the stone, but the ropes cut into her waist, holding her fast. Another flash of light from the window illuminated Randolph's body. She squeezed her eyes shut.

Whispers roused her. She opened her eyes and surveyed the warehouse. Randolph was gone, never to stir again. Shaw was silent as he watched the destruction of London. So why did she hear whispering?

She squeezed her eyes shut and concentrated. The words sounded over and over in her mind.

George William Frederick.

The king. The whispering repeated the name of the king. Was it the stone? As the Stone of Destiny, it was supposed to speak the name of the true king. Not Shaw's name, obviously, but Shaw didn't care about being the true king—he had just wanted to rouse the dragon. Did that mean it would take the true king to stop the chaos dragon?

But the king had been driven mad by the poisoning of his dragon. Even if they could somehow bring the stone to him, would he understand enough to sit on it and calm the chaos dragon?

Maybe the Prince Regent could do it. But then, he wasn't king yet, and if a claim to the throne was all that was needed, Amelia should have been able to do something as well, distant though her claim was.

She concentrated, but all she heard was *George William Frederick.*

She huffed. Stupid stone. Why did it have to be King George alone? He was descended from James Stuart, king of Scotland, but so were many other potential contenders for the crown. The Hanoverian Georges had been selected by Parliament to rule instead of the Catholic Stuarts as a matter of religion. Didn't that matter? Was it really destiny? Were they all just trapped in the roles they were given? Amelia didn't like to think so, but bound in a warehouse while a dragon battle raged on the Thames, it was hard for her to argue otherwise.

If the stone wanted the king, then, it would be disappointed. His mind was broken, along with his health. The government was in a regency with no true king. There was no one to control the chaos dragon.

Not until Shaw wiped out the royal family and had himself installed as ruler. If that happened, would it mean it was his destiny?

Amelia was tired of destiny. Tired of the roles she had been given as unwanted younger daughter. Family burden. Social pariah. She had tried to break out of them by creating Miss Charity, but that had failed. She needed to find a way to rewrite her destiny.

Lightning split the darkness. Whatever magic was at work over the Thames, it was powerful. Thunder followed the bright flash. No, it was the roar of a dragon. Amelia's heart quickened. A very large, fierce dragon. They were fighting in more earnest now.

As if offering Amelia a sign, several flashes of lightning in a row cast a lingering light, allowing her to see the warehouse more clearly for a moment. Her breath caught when she realized what was stacked near her. Kegs of gunpowder. No doubt some of them were used on Westminster Palace, and the rest were destined for other targets.

If Amelia could ignite them, she could destroy Shaw and all of his plans. Maybe destroy the Stone of Destiny as well.

Of course, it would also kill her. She didn't wish to die, but her life seemed paltry in comparison with the lives of so many important people. The destiny of her country. Those few people she called friends.

And who would miss Amelia? An image of Blackerby's laughing eyes flashed in her mind, but she pushed that aside. He would hardly notice she was gone. She had never been good enough to be loved. Her family certainly didn't care for her. Gentlemen had no interest in her. But Millicent and Phoebe, with their attunement to light, had seen something worthwhile in her, and now Shaw threatened to steal their happy futures. Amelia would deny him his victory.

She gritted her teeth against the stinging pain and wrenched her hands in opposite directions. The rope scraped her raw wounds, and she choked back a scream. Tears welled in her eyes. She ignored the burning in her shoulders and the agony tingling up her arms and yanked again. It felt as though she were peeling the skin from her hands. One more tug, and her hands pulled free.

She stifled a gasp and looked down at her hands, throbbing red and smeared with blood. Her fingers tingled with pins and needles, and she could barely move them. Shaw kept his back to her. Choking back a sob, she tried to work loose the knots holding her to the Stone of Scone, but her prickling hands wouldn't obey.

Another blast of light washed over the warehouse, showing her Randolph's body. He might have had a knife or something else useful. She made certain Shaw was distracted watching the fight through the spyglass then waited for the light from outside to fade. In the dimness, she reached forward, pulling against the ropes tight around her midsection, and felt Randolph's still-warm body. She shuddered and swallowed the bile in her throat, forcing herself to search his pockets with clumsy hands. Her fingers brushed the cold barrel of a pistol hidden in his coat. Perhaps the same pistol that he had leveled at her head on several occasions.

She pulled the pistol behind her, as if her hands were still tied, in case Shaw looked in her direction. It would be easy to fire at him, but she had never shot a gun before and was likely to miss. Then Shaw would tie her up again, or perhaps knock her senseless. That was no good.

But a pistol could certainly make a spark. If she shot it into one of the barrels of gunpowder, she might be able to set off an explosion and save her friends. She clutched the gun in her hands, the metal warming under her fingers. Lady Amelia Chase would finally be of use to someone.

Chapter Twenty-Two

SHADOWS ENCIRCLED Blackerby as he walked down the narrow streets of the docks, teasing him, mocking him.

Failure. Too late. Failure. Too late.

The shadows echoed the sounds of the battle raging before the Tower as the White Dragon and the dragon-linked held back the chaos dragon, slowly losing ground. They echoed the sounds of a gunshot, the dying gasps of…

Of someone.

Not Amelia, he prayed. The thought that he might already be too late wracked Blackerby with a pain that surprised him. He did not like the idea of a world without Amelia Chase in it.

He stopped and reached out through the thick shadows that wound around warehouses and breweries. But the chaos wove its way through, confusing the echoes in the darkness. He suspected Shaw was close, but he couldn't discern anything. Not Shaw. And not Amelia.

"Find her," he said to Shade.

If she was close, the dragon could lead Blackerby to her and Shaw both.

Blackerby followed Shade's silent, swooping figure through the streets. One of the chaos dragon's tentacles crashed down on a building along the riverbank nearby, crumbling it. Blackerby hesitated. How close was Shaw to the dragon? It didn't matter. Blackerby jogged onward, following the dark form of Shade against the magic-bright night.

They passed London Bridge, making their way deeper into the assortment of merchants' halls, breweries, wharves, and warehouses huddled along the edge of the river.

Shade fluttered lower and perched near the window of one of the warehouses. Blackerby approached warily and stopped to feel what the shadows told him.

Fear. Anger. Death.

Very recent death, the echoes of the gunshot still in the air.

Blackerby thought of Lady Amelia gone, and a gaping, empty place opened inside of him. The shadows crowded around him, whispering promises of strength. Of revenge.

He dropped his defenses and let the shadows in. All of them. Darkness and chittering secrets took over his heart and mind. And he slammed against the warehouse door, splintering it wide. Doors did not stop darkness. People had been trying to lock it out since there were humans to fear the dark, but they couldn't lock it out. Not out of their houses. Not out of their hearts and minds. And the darkness loved Shaw. Nothing would keep it away from him now.

Amelia had nearly worked up the courage to pull the trigger and ignite the gunpowder when the door to the warehouse burst open. A figure stood there in the doorway—a figure made of blackness, a darkness almost impossible to focus on. But she made herself look and gasped. It was Blackerby, but as she had never seen him before. His eyes were entirely black, and the darkness drifted off his skin like smoke from a fire within.

Shaw turned from the window, inhaled sharply, and took a step back.

So, there was something he feared after all. Or, at least he could be startled.

"Shaw," Blackerby said, though his voice hissed, not his own, and the sound of it reverberated through the vibrating shadows of the warehouse and even outside, as though a taut harp string ran from Blackerby through all the darkness in London.

Shaw straightened. "Lord Blackerby, I believe. Our paths cross again." He held out a hand as Blackerby moved forward. "I would not move if I were you. I have something here that you value."

Shaw gestured to Amelia. She scoffed at him. Blackerby would sacrifice her to destroy Shaw, and she understood—England depended on it.

"The stone is here!" Amelia called. "We can stop Shaw."

Blackerby raised his eyes to her, and something in them changed. The black contracted, making them look human again, though unnaturally dark. Blackerby was still in there. Amelia raised the gun slightly so he could see it. He shook his head and returned his attention to Shaw.

"You are under arrest," Blackerby announced to Shaw. His voice, though raspy, sounded more like his own.

"I don't think I am. Not with the chaos dragon still at large. The only one who can bring it under control is the rightful king, and yours is not of sound mind. Unless you're willing to kill him and let Prinny take the throne. Do you trust him with the power of the chaos dragon? No? You could eliminate him, too, and allow Princess Charlotte to reign. But how much are you willing to sacrifice?"

Amelia watched Blackerby, saw the hesitation on his face. The shadows quivered and roiled through the warehouse.

Shaw smiled. "Have you ever thought that this is not your destiny —being a lackey for a mad king and an idiot prince? This is not England's destiny. We both know it could be better. Your destiny is here, with me. Darkness and chaos are the perfect pairing. Don't you feel it?"

Blackerby's shoulders sagged. Anxious shadows washed around Amelia like waves.

"Blackerby!" she called. "You can choose your destiny! You understand the darkness, but it is not you."

His eyes brightened at that, animation coming back into his face.

Shaw whirled on Amelia, fury in his eyes. "I will kill you and let your blood run into the stone. Then the chaos dragon will never sleep."

Amelia tightened her grip on the pistol. If she fired it, she might set off the gunpowder as well.

"You won't touch her." Blackerby's voice filled the room, deep and commanding.

Shaw froze.

Blackerby went on. "Lady Amelia told me something interesting once, Shaw. She told me that sometimes it takes darkness to see the light. I wonder if that is what darkness is for—to show us where the light is. Shall we see if there is any light left in you? The darkness is certainly hungry to greet you."

Shaw's face went pale, his expression uncertain. Blackerby lifted his arms, and the darkness ran off of him, flowing away like water pooling toward Shaw. Shaw stared, watching it come, almost as if he was curious himself what it would do to him.

The shadows twisted around Shaw, clinging to him, and he screamed. Writhed. Amelia wanted to look away, but she couldn't. All she could see was the horror etched over Shaw's face as the darkness seeped into him, seeped in through the many cracks he had opened in himself over the years.

Blackerby ran up to her. "Don't watch, my dear," he whispered, shielding her from the sight.

She turned her gaze to him, relieved to see his eyes their usual brown, though there was no mocking in them now. He placed a gentle hand on her cheek, as she leaned her face into his reassuring touch. He frowned at the ropes binding her to the stone, then he grabbed one of the iron rings and twisted it sharply, jolting Amelia and pulling the ring free. He lifted the ropes off of her.

Amelia took a deep breath, dizzy with relief and exhaustion. Blackerby put his arms out to steady her, and she gladly let herself fall into them. He wrapped her close and held her against his chest, and she breathed in the scent of sandalwood and listened to the rapid beating of his heart. Safe. Protected.

But it couldn't last. The rumbles of fighting continued outside. She looked up to find Blackerby watching her with a curious, almost tender expression. A blush warmed her cheeks, and she lowered her eyes.

"We have to try destroying the stone," Amelia said. "Maybe then the chaos dragon will sleep."

Blackerby released her slowly and faced the stone: large and rough-hewn, but otherwise innocent-looking.

Blackerby ran his fingers over its surface. "Easily enough done. It's only limestone. I don't know if it will work, but I'm willing to try."

He lifted a crowbar from against the wall. In one solid strike, the Stone of Scone split into several pieces.

Another flash of lightning tore across the night.

Amelia groaned. "It didn't do anything, did it?"

Blackerby frowned at the broken pieces of stone. "I think breaking it may prevent anyone from using the dragon this way in the future, but for the present, the king has to calm the dragon."

"But can he?" Amelia asked.

A rasping breath drew their attention back to Shaw. The shadows fell away from him, and he collapsed to the floor like a marionette with its strings cut. Blackerby squeezed Amelia's arm then walked over to kneel by Shaw.

"He's dead."

Amelia let her breath out in a burst. "You're certain?"

"Oh, yes. I guess there was no light left in him after all."

"He must not have always been so... empty. He told me he was protecting his family."

Blackerby stood and dusted off his hands. "Possibly at one point, his intentions were not all selfish, but he let darkness consume him. You were right, my dear: we can choose what we will be, and he chose darkness. So, when it came for him, he had nothing left to fight it with." He turned back to her. "I nearly let it happen to me as well, but I found there was some light left in me. And you were part of that."

"Me?" Amelia flushed.

"You reminded me of the good parts of myself."

She looked away. "Then I am glad." Her gaze fell on the broken stone. "What are we to do about that?"

Blackerby picked up one of the smaller chunks of the stone. He tossed it up and caught it. "We're going to visit His Majesty. If there is any light left in his mind, we will coax it out of him."

Amelia hesitated, but Blackerby took her hand and hurried her out of the warehouse.

"We need a horse," Blackerby said. "A fast one. The sooner we end this, the better chance of saving our friends at the Tower. I—"

He stopped and cocked his head as though listening. Then, astonishment brightened his eyes, and he squeezed Amelia's hand. "Perhaps luck *is* an element."

"What?"

"Unless the shadows are deceiving me, the king is riding to the Tower. Hurry!"

They raced back along the streets, and the turrets of the White Tower came into view.

The Byward Tower had collapsed, and the White Dragon struggled with the chaos dragon on the banks of the Thames. The chaos dragon's tentacles lashed around the White Dragon's neck and constricted. The White Dragon reared back, and they crashed into the wharf, sending splinters of wood and chunks of ice and water blasting into the air and showering down.

Amelia caught a glimpse of the dragon-linked huddled behind a chunk of fallen tower. Lord Westing's white-blond hair stood out in the dark. At his gesture, ice swarmed out and clung to one of the chaos dragon's tentacles. A wave from the river battered the creature, forcing it to release the White Dragon.

"Make way!"

She whirled to see a contingent of Bow Street Runners clearing the streets of the few onlookers brave enough to come this close to the dragon battle.

A coach-and-six escorted by blue-coated cavalrymen clattered over the stones behind them. Blackerby tugged at Amelia's arm, and they hurried over to it.

Joshua and Brainy Jamie rushed up to meet them, both grinning widely.

"We brought reinforcements!" Joshua declared, puffing his chest.

"We 'elped the Runners clear the streets better than a sweep ever could," Brainy Jamie said with a winded laugh.

"So you did." Blackerby pulled Amelia forward to meet the coach.

The guards clustered to stop Blackerby but fell back when they recognized him.

Queen Charlotte opened the coach's curtains and peered out. "Lord Blackerby! Tell me why my husband is shouting that he must come to the Tower. He was near to hurting himself in his excitement, so I did not know what to do but bring him hither."

Blackerby bowed low. "Your Majesty. He is answering the call of the White Dragon. England is under attack, and His Majesty is the only one who can stop it."

She glanced over her shoulder into the dark recesses of the coach. "He is not well, you realize—unable to do much. I do not know that he will be of any use."

Blackerby looked uncertain as well. Amelia cleared her throat and curtseyed deeply.

"Your Majesty, if I may. His use is not in what he can do, but in the light that resides in him."

Blackerby smiled at her. "Indeed. If he was responsive enough to obey the dragon's call, we must believe he can still save his kingdom."

The queen tilted her head, then nodded once. She opened the door of the coach and summoned them to approach.

Amelia followed close behind Blackerby, stopping at the coach door. Only dim light reached inside, but she could make out the king's form: an old man, crippled by pain, his unseeing eyes squinting, and his face mostly hidden by a long, white beard. A pale, emaciated dragon stretched across his lap.

Blackerby glanced at Amelia, his eyes uncertain, then held out the piece of the Stone of Scone for the king.

"Your Majesty," he said loudly. "You must take this stone and command the elements to be still."

"Eh?" the king called, bending an ear closer. "Still? Darkness is still. Death is still."

Blackerby shifted his grip on the stone and cleared his throat. "Command the chaos to be calm, Your Majesty."

The king smacked his lips and wrinkled his forehead, but he did not reach for the stone.

It had been several years since her presentation at court, but Amelia had never had a particular shyness of Their Majesties, and even less so seeing the king so much like one of her elderly cousins. She put a hand on Blackerby's arm and squeezed up beside him in the coach's doorway. His closeness distracted her for a moment, but she placed her fingers alongside Blackerby's on the stone. He released it and placed his hand on Amelia's back, flooding her with warmth.

She turned the stone over in her hand and then lowered it so the king could feel its rough surface. He took it from her and clutched it tightly.

Blackerby moved as if he would speak, but Amelia shook her head and gestured for him to stay quiet.

"George William Frederick," the king said, looking blindly around the coach. "Did you hear that? That used to be me so very long ago. What a strange rock. It almost makes me remember."

"Wish for peace," Amelia called. "Peace, Your Majesty."

The king's face relaxed. "Peace. Yes, peace is a treasure I long for."

An enormous splash sounded behind them, and the whole group—except the king—turned to see the ripples splashing against the bank where the chaos dragon had sunk into the waters. The White Dragon shook itself and limped onto the bank.

"He stopped it!" Amelia said, throwing her arms around Blackerby.

He returned the embrace, holding her fiercely.

"Well," Her Majesty said, an eyebrow raised.

Amelia moved to pull away, but Blackerby held her close still.

"Your Majesty," he said to the queen, "I believe His Majesty has earned his rest."

Indeed, the king seemed to have sunk into a slumber. The piece of the Stone of Scone tumbled from his fingers, and Blackerby snatched it from the floor of the coach.

The queen sighed, a deep weariness stealing into her eyes. "I imagine we all have."

Blackerby bowed and guided Amelia back from the royal coach.

The guards surrounded it again, and it rattled back over the stones. The Runners stayed to guard the damaged wall of the Tower.

The dragon-linked began to step warily from behind their shelter, as if uncertain whether the battle was truly over. Amelia glanced down at the stone in Blackerby's fingers.

"What are you going to do with that, and the rest of the stone?"

Blackerby considered for a moment. "We will return it to Scotland, secretly, and introduce a forgery to sit in Westminster Abbey."

"You think that's right?"

"I do. The chaos dragon can sleep under the mud of the Thames for all of time. Chaos may be a part of life, but we don't need it stirring. And the stone belongs to Scotland anyway. No one need be the wiser. Prinny does not need access to a chaos dragon, and whatever His Majesty might say of what he felt when he held the stone, everyone will dismiss it as part of his madness."

"True," she said, feeling very sorry for the mad old king.

"Come," Blackerby took her arm. "We must tell the dragon-linked how the king commanded the chaos dragon and see if any are injured, though I believe the White Dragon took the brunt of the attack. We will have to repair his resting place so he can recover. The Luddites may not disappear entirely, but we have cut off their head, and I foresee greater peace ahead for us."

He started forward, nearly dragging her over the uneven stones.

Amelia tugged her arm free from his. "I don't think I should go back. I'll not be welcome in Society now. Not after Miss Charity."

He reached his hand out for her. "If we ignore that scandal, people will begin to doubt it."

"You think so?"

"My dear, I know the ways of secrets. Besides, it will make for much more shocking gossip when you become the Countess of Blackerby."

Her cheeks reddened. "You do not have to marry me to appease my father."

"I would never do anything to appease your father. But I don't plan to marry you to annoy him, either. That will only be the cream on the cake. I want to marry you because I can't imagine how dull life would be without you."

Amelia started and looked up at him. "You cannot mean it."

"I do, my dear trickster." He ran a finger down her cheek, and she shivered at his gentle touch. "Say you won't leave me, my light in the dark."

She met his eyes, and her throat tightened at the tenderness she saw in them. A smile spread over her face. "Never, my lord jester."

The laughter returned to his eyes. "I'm glad that's settled, then. I consider this night a complete victory. Well, no, not quite complete."

"What's left?" Amelia asked.

"Only this."

He pulled her in and brought his lips down to hers, warm and intense and banishing all other worries from her mind. A complete victory indeed.

Author's Note

Thank you for joining me for this adventure in an alternate Regency England. Though this is a work of historical fantasy, I have tried to stay as accurate as possible when it came to details and events in the books. In this book in particular, however, I did rearrange some events to be influenced by the magical happenings in this version of London.

The old Westminster Palace did burn down, though it occurred in 1834 when a fire set in the lower parts of the building burned out of control—it was an accident and not an attack by Luddites or other anti-government organizations (though they did riot elsewhere). It's true that the House of Commons turned their noses up at the offer to meet at Buckingham Palace, which was not transformed into the premier royal residence until Queen Victoria's reign.

Spencer Perceval was the only British Prime Minister (to date, and hopefully ever) to be assassinated. He was shot by a lone anti-government protester in 1812, a year earlier than the fantasy setting of this book.

King George III's mental and physical breakdown, and his son's rule as Prince Regent, is well known by many interested in this era. By 1813, the king was blind, mostly deaf, crippled by rheumatism, and very rarely aware of what was happening around him. The exact cause of his affliction is unknown (as the real King George didn't have a dragon to poison), though various theories have suggested arsenic poisoning, the blood disease porphyria, and bipolar disorder.

And the Stone of Scone or Stone of Destiny has been the subject of several controversies and conspiracies. Some people doubt the real stone ever left Scotland, suggesting that the stone Edward I (Longshanks) took back to England with him was a fake, switched out by Scottish monks. And in 1950, a group of Scottish students broke into Westminster Abbey and stole the Stone of Scone, accidentally breaking it in half in the process. They later returned the repaired stone to an abbey in Scotland, but there have been rumors ever since that the stone they returned was not the original. The stone was sent back to Westminster Abbey, but later moved officially to Scotland. At this point, no one knows if the stone is the real one, though perhaps if one sat on it, they would be able to hear it whisper the name of the true king as legends state.

As much as possible, I have used real myths and legends from British history in creating the lore of this alternate world. Ancient British tales said the head of Bran the Blessed was buried under the hill on which the White Tower of the Tower of London stands, and that its presence helped protect Britain from its enemies. "Bran" is Welsh for raven, and legends state that if the ravens ever leave the Tower of London, then the Tower and the kingdom will fall. I have replaced Bran's head in this instance with the White Dragon, a symbol of England and the Saxons in ancient tales that pit the English White Dragon against the Red Dragon of Wales.

Other Books by E.B. Wheeler

British Fiction:

The Haunting of Springett Hall

Born to Treason

The Royalist's Daughter

Wishwood (Westwood Gothic)

Moon Hollow (Westwood Gothic)

Utah Fiction:

No Peace with the Dawn (with Jeffery Bateman)

Bootleggers and Basil (in *The Pathways to the Heart*)

Letters from the Homefront

Balm of the Heart (in *In the Valley*)

Blood in a Dry Town (Tenny Mateo Mystery)

The Bone Map

Acknowledgments

Thank you to my critique groups, the Cache Valley Chapter of the League of Utah Writers and UPSSEFW, and to my beta readers, Dan, Karen, Lauren, Melanie, and Rosario, for helping to bring out the best in my books and making writing a less lonely process. And as always, I couldn't do this without the understanding, patience, and support of my family.

About the Author

E.B. Wheeler attended BYU, majoring in history with an English minor, and earned graduate degrees in history and landscape architecture from Utah State University. She's the award-winning author of over a dozen books, including Whitney Award finalists *A Proper Dragon* and *Born to Treason,* as well as several short stories, magazine articles, and scripts for educational software programs. The League of Utah Writers named her the Writer of the Year in 2016. In addition to writing, she consults about historic preservation and teaches history.

Find more about her and her books at ebwheeler.com

Made in the USA
Las Vegas, NV
18 May 2022

49051451R00105